A CASINO CURSED

A CASINO CURSED

FRANK BEHR

A Casino Cursed

Copyright © 2023 by Frank Behr. All rights reserved.

No part of this publication may be reproduced, stored in a retrieval system or transmitted in any way by any means, electronic, mechanical, photocopy, recording or otherwise without the prior permission of the author except as provided by USA copyright law.

The opinions expressed by the author are not necessarily those of URLink Print and Media.

1603 Capitol Ave., Suite 310 Cheyenne, Wyoming USA 82001
1-888-980-6523 | admin@urlinkpublishing.com

URLink Print and Media is committed to excellence in the publishing industry.

Book design copyright © 2023 by URLink Print and Media. All rights reserved.

Published in the United States of America

Library of Congress Control Number: 2023915879
ISBN 978-1-68486-612-0 (Paperback)
ISBN 978-1-68486-497-3 (Digital)

10.08.23

Chapter

1

THE SHOOTING

Darnell, Nevada is a new somewhat upscale subdivision in Henderson just off I-15 West where Derrick and Robyn Burns have lived for the past three years. The outside of the house is desert landscaped, of course, with a view of mountains off in the distance. They have a nice one level home that has two bedrooms, two full baths, an office nook and a kitchen that looks into the living room. They both work at the Starbrite Casino in Las Vegas. She works in event planning, and Derrick is a gaming supervisor. Robyn is just getting home from work. After parking her red Mazda 3 in the garage, she picked up the newspaper, mail, and then went inside. It is just before 5 pm, and she knew there was about an hour before Derrick got home. It's Nevada; it's August; it's triple digit hot. As usual when getting home from work, Robyn quickly went directly into the bedroom and stripped off her clothes. She opened a dresser drawer, put on a mini white bikini, picked up a towel, and headed for the pool.

Now Robyn is a stunning, nicely tanned, blond, blue-eyed model figured gal at 31. She is an absolute knockout in her bikini, and she knows it. The pool is moderate in size, just off the covered patio. Robyn walked down the pool steps and swam around for ten or fifteen minutes trying not to get her shoulder-length hair wet. The water is never cold but just cool enough to feel refreshing. As she was stepping out of the pool she said to herself, "Wow, just what I needed!" She opened the patio door into the kitchen, grabbed a cold can of Bud Light, picked up the newspaper and headed back outside to sit under the canopy covered deck.

Robyn knew she still had about a half hour left before Derrick would get home and would probably want to go out for dinner and a couple of drinks, as they usually did on Wednesday evenings. In the hot shade under the patio roof it would not take long to dry off. She took a swig of her Bud Light and opened the newspaper. Front page showed Lucky Oasis Casino Shooting. The casino is located on I-15 just north of Jean and is owned by Jack Capano, a close friend of theirs. She continued reading and found out it was an apparent botched robbery with Jack being shot as the two robbers escaped. Sitting up she said, "Ohh shit" and continued reading finding out Jack was taken to Desert View Hospital in critical condition. She stood up, gulped her beer and went inside to get dressed.

Derrick is a brown haired, 34 year old, handsome shaved guy that works out to stay in shape. He is a well built 6 foot one guy that enjoys being a gaming supervisor at the Starbrite Casino. He met his wife Robyn about four years ago there. They both hit it off immediately and got married about a year after they met. Together they earn enough money to support their active lifestyle. When Robyn's grandfather passed away six months after their wedding, she inherited a large sum that they used to buy the home in Darnell.

Derrick pulled into his driveway and parked his silver Subaru Forester inside the garage. It was almost 6:15pm, and he was tired after a tedious day supervising dealers and various problems and could not wait to get home and relax.

Just as Derrick opened his house door he was greeted by a hug and kiss from Robyn. Whooa, what is that all about he thought as he usually just gets a quick peck on the lips? She said, "I've got some sad news about your friend Jack." "What's the sad news?" Derrick asked.

"Why don't you sit down, take your shoes off, relax, and I will get you a beer first," she suggested.

"Well that is nice of you; must be really sad news," as he flopped down on the couch and kicked off his shoes. Robyn gave Derrick a Bud and sat down next to him with the newspaper in hand. "Here, look at the headlines." Derrick grabbed the newspaper and saw the story about the attempted robbery of the Lucky Oasis Casino and the shooting of Jack that said he was in critical condition. "What the hell is this!" he shouted. Jack shot? In critical condition?"

Robyn started to shed some tears as Derrick finished reading. The paper went on to say that the police were investigating the shooting. They are reviewing the security tapes to see what the two men looked like. At present, no one has been charged, nor do they have any suspects. No other details were available.

Derrick flipped the paper on the couch saying "I'm going to call the hospital and see if I can get anymore information on Jack."

"Yes! I was going to do just that but I heard you pull into the garage and waited for you instead. Here is the phone number."

Derrick pulled out his cell phone and dialed the hospital. "Desert View Hospital how may I help you?"

"I just read in the newspaper that my good friend Jack Capano was shot and is in critical condition. Can I come in to visit him, or is he able to talk on the phone?" he asked. "Just one minute, please."

About two minutes later the person at the hospital said, "I am sorry, but no one can visit or talk on the phone with him at this time."

"That's what I figured and thanks for your time." Derrick hung up. "Robyn, I 'm going to call Steve at the Oasis and see if he can give me any news." Now Steve was not exactly a friend of his or of Robyn but he knew Steve was the manager of the Oasis so he called him.

"Lucky Oasis Casino and Lodge," answered a pleasant voiced gal.

"I would like to talk with Steve Conti please."

"Sorry, she answered, Steve is not in right now. If you give me your name and phone number, I will give it to Steve when he gets in."

"Aaah, do you know anything about what happened yesterday?" asked Derrick.

"What do you mean, do I know anything?"

"Listen, my name is Derrick Burns. Jack Capano and I are long time good friends, and I am just trying to find out what took place. What is your name?"

"My name is Rosy, Mr. Burns. I just started here two weeks ago as the phone greeter. The only thing I know and can say is that two guys came in, went up into Jack's office and shot him. I do not know if the two guys wanted to rob us or not. I can tell you that Jack was taken to the Desert View Hospital. Do you know where that is?"

"Yes Rosy, I do. Thank you for what you could give me, and I will try and call or even stop in later. Keep the Oasis in good spirits, Rosy" as Derrick hung up.

He looked at Robyn and said, "I could not get in contact with Steve, and Rosy, the new phone greeter, could not give me any real details other than what we read in the newspaper. Jack cannot have visitors or talk on the phone. This does not sound good. Maybe I should go down to the Oasis tomorrow and see what I can find out. I think I will call Starbrite tomorrow and see if I can come in a little late."

Robyn with a worried look said, "Yea, does sound really screwed up to me too. I can't see what else we can do about it this evening. Do you think we should go out to our regular Wednesday dinner tonite?"

Derrick looked at his watch, it was about 6:45 and said, "Why not?" We need to eat and it's getting late, plus we need to relax our minds on this whole thing."

Derrick changed into his casual clothes and off they went to dinner.

It was Thursday 7am when the alarm went off. Derrick and Robyn both got out of bed on each side. "Want to take a shower with me?" asked Derrick.

"Of course. That is the best way to save on water. We just need to be quick about it. No fucking around," responded Robyn.

"Who me?" Robyn just smiled and got into the shower. She pressed her perfectly firm breasts against his hairy chest kissing him. "Turn around," she said and then washed his back. She then spun him around kissing him again while she grabbed and wash his man thing. "Didn't you say no fucking around?" "Shut up and relax," she instructed.

It did not take Derrick long to reach his climax. He kissed her again. While he was washing Robyn's back and said, "I will take care of you later."

"You better," she said.

Derrick got out of the shower. Quickly dried off and put on his business suit. He then called the Starbrite Casino informing them he needed to come in two hours late."

Getting ready for work did not take Robyn more than a half hour. Since she was a natural beauty she used a moderate amount of makeup and brushed her now dry, somewhat wavy blond hair without much thought to neatness. She liked her hair to be a little messy anyway. She was just walking out of the bathroom as Derrick came in. "No problem getting to work a couple hours late," he said. Robyn nodded and headed to the kitchen to put on some coffee.

"Want eggs or pancakes or just brownies?" she shouted.

"Just a brownie and coffee would be fine," he answered.

Derrick thanked Robyn for getting the coffee and brownie. He kissed her and said, "I'll call you at work if I find something out at the Oasis." He turned off the television after reviewing the morning traffic report. All traffic was moving freely, including I-15, with no jam ups. He got in his Forester heading out to the Lucky Oasis. Derrick figured he had about one hour to spend at the Oasis before he needed to leave.

The Lucky Oasis Casino and Lodge is on I-15 north of Jean and is the last casino before hitting Las Vegas. Generally they did a very steady business, mainly from locals and those traveling from California going to Las Vegas. It is a friendly place to unwind and enjoy light meals. The lodge has twenty low-priced units mainly for convenience of those having too much to drink or couples having a one night fling. All units were on the backside of the casino and connected without going outside. The first two units were never rented as the owner Jack Capano used them for an office and his housing.

As Derrick pulled into the parking lot in front of the casino, he noticed few vehicles. The Oasis was never jam packed except on Friday and Saturday nights when they have live country and western bands. They were upcoming local bands that were very well supported. Derrick entered by the front casino entrance and went over to the cashier asking where Steve was. "He should be in the office," the cashier girl said. So he headed straight to the casino office noticing a hand full of slot players and two people playing blackjack.

Steve Conti was going through files in a stand up cabinet. Steve looks like he could be Indian but is a dark tanned Italian, forty two year old with thick wavy black hair showing some gray. He stands about five foot nine inches with an average build, wearing a short sleeve shirt exposing his tatoos on both arms that looked like some type of snake. He is not a very sociable type guy and likes to get straight to the point. He noticed Derrick walking to the stairs of the second floor office. The office overlooked the entire casino floor with its wall to wall, floor to ceiling one- way glass windows. "Well hi there stranger," he said as he had not seen Derrick in quite some time. "Howdy," replied Derrick.

"How is your knock out wife doing?"

"She's fine, Steve, but I really don't have a lot of time as I need to get to work. I just wanted to stop in and ask you about what I read in the newspaper saying Jack was shot here.

"Yes, Tuesday. Here have a seat. Would you like something to drink?"

"No, I'm okay."

"Let me say that this is very upsetting to me and all those working here. We all love Jack. He is a great person to work for, and we hope he pulls through. I know Jack was a friend of yours, and I am sorry for what happened."

"Can you give me any more details on this shooting?" asked Derrick.

"Probably not much more than what you read in the paper. But here is what took place. I was fixing one of the slots when I heard the shots and looked up to the office and saw two guys running out down the stairs. By the time I got to the office stairs the two guys were gone fleeing out by the side entrance. I then went up to the office and saw Jack lying on the floor. Right here (as he pointed to a spot next to the desk) with a lot of blood on his shirt. He was not dead, but he was breathing heavily and I could tell he was in a great deal of pain. Two or three workers were now coming into the office. I shouted out, 'Call 911 and get me some towels,' as I put a desk seat cushion under Jack's head."

Steve continued, "It took the ambulance about 10 minutes to get here. They quickly ripped opened Jack's shirt to apply large gauze pads to where he suffered two gunshot wounds to his chest, and taped him up to stop the bleeding. The police arrived just then and cleared everyone, except me, out of the office. I explained what happened to the police as the paramedics put Jack on a stretcher and carried him out to the ambulance. They took Jack to the Desert View Hospital."

"So he was shot twice. Was this a robbery or just a random shooting or what?" Derrick asked.

"Yes, he was shot twice. I think they wanted to rob the place because the top desk drawer was opened where the keys to the counting room and Jack's .38 Special were kept. So when they saw him trying to grab the gun, they just shot him and ran.

Two detectives and a crime-scene investigator came in just after the police arrived and found two shell casings on the floor. They asked me the same questions you asked. They inspected Jack's gun that was also on the floor and looked around the office while dusting for any finger prints. One detective asked me if I knew in what type of car they drove off. They also questioned a couple of the employees. When the detectives were ready to leave, they said an investigation will be made and they would be in touch soon. That's about what happened Derrick."

"Well, thanks Steve, for the information. I certainly hope Jack makes it, and I will try to call the hospital later to hear how he is doing. I have to get to work now but will see you again soon. Keep me informed. Here is my cell number. If you hear anything at all, please just give a call and keep the Oasis going."

"That is what I am doing and have been doing," Steve reacted. Derrick thought the tone of the response was somewhat bold but thought it might just be all the stress and anxiety he was going through.

Derrick arrived at the Starbrite Casino just before 10am. He went right to pit two where he is scheduled to work. He is not the pit boss but head of the supervisors in that pit. Already the action was picking up with several players at the tables. It is Thursday, the start of many conventions, and they expect a full house for the entire weekend. The pit boss, Gus, is a very likeable, easy going guy. Seeing Derrick coming in he asked how his friend was doing. "He is in critical condition," answered Derrick.

"Sorry to hear that," Gus said. "Do you think you could work Saturday?" asked Gus. Derrick said, "Yes. Could I have next Monday off?" Gus agreed. Derrick worked an extra hour, until 6pm, making up one of the two hours when he started late in the morning. When he got home, he planned on calling the hospital again for Jack's condition.

As Derrick was approaching his SUV in the gargage his phone rang. "Derrick, this is Steve."

"Yes Steve, what's up?"

"Got bad news. Jack did not make it. I just received the news from the hospital that he died about three hours ago."

"Ohh fuck!" Derrick said in shock. "That's just unbelievable!"

"When I find out any more details, I'll let you know."

Derrick shaking his head sighed and dejectedly said, "I can't believe this happened. Any more details?"

"Again. Let me find out what arrangements need to be made, and I will let you know."

"Alright," Derrick hung up. He opened the drivers door to his SUV and just sat there quietly for about 15 minutes before heading home.

Derrick walked slowly into his house and looked for Robyn. He didn't see her at first, but then saw the smoke through the patio doors and went outside. Robyn was trying to keep the hamburgers warm on the upper part of the grill as they were done ten minutes ago. "I was wondering when you were going to get home.

The hamburgers are more than done and you didn't call me today." She noticed Derrick just standing by the patio door with his mouth open looking very sad.

"Jack did not make it Robyn," as he burst out crying.

"Oh my God," she replied and put her arms around Derrick and they both wept together.

Chapter

2

THE FUNERAL

After crying their eyes out, they both seated themselves on the couch with Robyn's head against his chest. "How did you find out? What's going to happen now? I mean as to the funeral and his casino?" asked Robyn.

"Steve called me about Jack as I was leaving the Starbrite and said he would get back to me with more details. As far as not calling you today about our meeting this morning, we were swamped due to the conventions starting and I did not get a chance. I *d*on't really know what will happen now. Jack doesn't have anyone left except his mother, and she is not in very good health."

Jack's mother Sophia is sixty seven years old and is suffering from rheumatoid arthritis. She rarely goes anywhere except with her girl friends and to the doctor.

She has never been involved with Jack's casino and was always happy when he visited her. Even though Derrick and Robyn haven't seen her in about a year, they felt they needed to give her a call.

"Hello," a weaken voice answered.

"Hi Sophia, this is Derrick Burns. You know, friend of Jack's."

"Oh, oh yes." she answered in a somber tone. "You calling about" her voice so week as Derrick weighed in "Yes, about Jack. I know it is just after 7pm Sophia, and you're probably not up to seeing anyone, but Robyn and I thought maybe you would want some company this evening." "Robyn?" like she didn't know. "Yes, my wife."

"Alright. I have my friend Joyce here now but she is about to leave. If you want to come, that's fine."

Sophia lives in a modest two bedroom home in Spring Valley which is about 25 miles from Derrick and Robyn's home. They arrived at 7:40pm ringing the door bell. Sophia opened the door and seeing that she had been crying Robyn put her arms around her. "I am so sorry about Jack," said Robyn with tears running down her cheeks. As they separated she noticed that she twinged and added, "Are you in pain, Sophia?"

"Oh its my arthritis. It's been killing me. You must be Robyn, Derrick's wife, right?" "Yes I am."

"Come on in. Have a seat on the couch. Would you like something to drink?"

Derrick answered, "No we are just fine. We wanted to come over and spend a little time with you and see how you are doing. Sorry it has been so long since we last been together. Last time, I think, was with Jack and we had a little cookout." Sophia didn't seem to remember that.

"You know, the way things have happened lately, when you called it didn't resgister to me who you were. I am glad that you both came to visit," the words coming out of Sophia's mouth in a quivery soft spoken way.

"How did you find out about Jack?" asked Derrick.

"When they took him to the hospital from the Lucky Oasis they were given my name and phone number, I guess. They were told I was his mother."

"You doing alright, Sophia? I mean is there anything we can do for you now?" asked Derrick. Silence. "I, I'm doing the best I can Derrick. You know Jack was my only child. He did visit me often and helped me out when I needed something. Ohhh, I'm goin' to miss my son!" With that she started weeping again. Robyn went over and put her arms around her. After gaining her composure she said, "I have several good girl friends, and we get together weekly. We are all widows now you know? However, this business of arranging for Jack's wake and funeral has me somewhat shaken."

Derrick looked at Robyn and said, "Why don't we help out with that? Is there a funeral home you like or want to use?"

"Well, yes, there's Mountain View Funeral Home not far from here in Spring Valley. Matthew Gordon owns it, and we have known each other for a long time. That would be the place I would like to use," Sophia said.

They both saw that Sophia was very tired and getting weaker. So Derrick said, "Alright, that is the funeral home we will contact for you if you want us to."

"Yes, I would like that very much."

"Sophia do you have any other family members we should contact?"

"No. They are all gone."

"We will need a short signed letter from you showing Jack's full name, date of birth, address and social security number with a few words stating we can act on your behalf in handling the funeral arrangements."

"Hold on." She went off to write the letter and gave it to Derrick. She also suggested it might be a good idea to to contact attorney, Al Watson. That is the attorney Jack used for his affairs and gave him the phone number.

"Do not worry about anything, Sophia. We will take care of all the arrangements and keep you informed. If we need your input on any other matter, we will be in contact. For now, just try to relax. If you are contacted by anyone you are not comfortable with, refer them to me or Robyn." They again hugged Sophia, and she thanked them again as they departed.

Friday morning Derrick called the Starbrite to inform them that his best friend had just died, and he would need that day off to make funeral arrangements and take care of other matters. He apologized asking for this request since they were going to have a busy weekend. Since Derrick was a good worker and rarely took any time off from his scheduled shift, he had no problem with the request. Robyn figured Derrick could handle the funeral arrangements on his own. She decided to go to work knowing she would need to have time off for the wake and funeral. She asked Derrick to call her when he had more details.

As soon as Robyn left, Derrick called the Mountain View Funeral Home and was able to get a 1pm appointment. He took advantage of the morning time to pay bills and get the office in order. Then he went out and stopped at Chick-Fil-A for a chicken breast sandwich before going to the funeral home.

Derrick always liked to be punctual as he arrived at the Mountain View Funeral Home and walked directly to where it said office. He hesitated before going in when the person seated at the desk stood up and said, "May I help you?" "I am Derrick Burns, and I made a 1pm appointment."

"Yes, yes, come right in. My name is Matt Gordon, and you mentioned the name of the deceased was Jack ahhh..."

"Jack Capano," cut in Derrick.

"Oh yes. He is the young man that was recently shot in his casino. Right?"

"Yes, the Lucky Oasis Casino near Jean is where it happened." Derrick answered and continued. "Jack was my best friend. Since he doesn't have any family members alive except his mother who is in her late sixties and suffers from rheumatoid arthritis, she asked me to handle all the arrangements. Here is a letter from her. It should say in it that she wanted to use your funeral home."

Mr. Gordon reviewed the letter saying. "This is good and I do trust you but is it possible I could call her? I need to discuss the obituary notice, type of casket, etc."

"Sure, that's fine. Maybe I should make the call to put her at ease," Derrick suggested.

"Here, take the phone and call her yourself and ask if she would talk with me briefly."

Derrick called and Sophia answered. Derrick explained he was at the funeral home making the arrangements for Jack but Mr. Gordon wanted to talk with her. So he handed the phone back to Mr. Gordon. Basically all he wanted to do is offer Sophia his condolences and said he would take care of everything and that she should not worry. He said he would call her later or even visit her if she wanted to talk about the obituary, type of casket and flower arrangements. She agreed and he then turned back to Derrick.

"Where is Jack now?" asked Mr. Gordon.

"He died yesterday, and I guess he is at the Desert View Hospital," said Derrick.

"That's just down the road from here. I'll call the hospital and see if he is still there or at the morgue. When would you like to have the wake or do you think I should ask Sophia?"

"Probably that would be best to ask Sophia, but as far as I am concerned as soon as possible. There really isn't anyone that is far away that I can think of that would come."

Mr. Gordon then said, "Well, this is Friday and it will take two or three days to get everything ready. We do not have any funerals coming up as we speak. I will ask Sophia and suggest next Tuesday."

"Sounds good to me. When you call Sophia, please let me know what was decided. Here is my cell number," said Derrick.

"Good. "And please, call me anytime if you have any questions."

The wake of Jack Capano was Tuesday from 3 to until 8pm. Derrick and Robyn picked up Sophia at 1:30 and went to the Mountain View Funeral Home early as is customary for family and close friends. The funeral home director, Matt Gordon, greeted them and showed the way to the parlor where Jack was laid out. It was nicely set up with three floor flowers on each side of the casket that Sophia picked out. There were a few pictures of Jack's life displayed on a table near the side wall. Derrick accompanied Sophia with Robyn next to him up to the casket. They paid their respects and said some prayers.

Sophia's eyes, full of tears, seated herself up front. Derrick knew it was painful for Sophia to stand up long with her arthritis. He suggested that she just stay seated, and he would stand with Robyn to greet the visitors. Mr. Gordon took Derrick and showed him the restrooms and the break room that offered coffee, juice, water, cookies and brownies. He would be in his office if needed.

Jack only had his mom as family and really didn't have a slew of friends so they did not expect a large crowd for his visitation. As they waited time passed away slowly. Sophia's girl friends came in just before three as they wanted to visit with her before she would get busy. One by one each paid their respects to Jack and came over and sat down by Sophia. She perked up and thanked each one for coming. As they were talking, Derrick and Robyn greeted some casino friends of Jack. In many cases they knew them also through their gaming connection. One very sharp dressed, older man entered and signed in. When he came over to pay his respects, Derrick greeted him. He said, "Sorry to hear about Jack. I am Jack's attorney, Al Watson. After I say a prayer for Jack, is it possible I could have a few words with you in private?"

"Sure, that'll be fine. Nice to meet you," said Derrick.

The attorney went over and greeted Sophia. "I'm glad you came Al!" as she was quite familiar with him. They talked for a few minutes then he came over to Derrick with Robyn by his side. "Looks like they did a good job with Jack. He was just too young for this to happen." Looking at Robyn he said, "Is this your wife?"

"Yes this is my wife, Robyn. And this is Mr. Watson—umm, Jacks attorney." "Is this a good time for us to talk briefly?" asked Mr. Watson.

Derrick looked around and didn't see any new people coming in so he said, "Robyn, Mr. Watson wants to see me on some matter; we will be in the break room. Could you hold the fort and stay with Sophia, greeting whomever comes in?"

"No problem. I will come and get you if needed," she answered.

As they walked over to the break room, Derrick wondered what the hell this was all about. "Want some coffee and cookies?" asked Derrick.

"Yes, just coffee, black please." They sat at a small table, and the lawyer pulled out an envelope from inside his suit coat. "I'm not going take up much of your time as I know you need to get back and help with Sophia. In this envelope is a letter that states what Jack wanted to happen in the case of his death. I am not going to open it at this time nor should you. Instead, please put this in your coat pocket and read it when you and your wife get home. As a follow up, and you will want a follow up, I need to see you and your wife in my office as soon as possible."

"Wholly shit! Do we have a problem?" blurted out Derrick.

"No, no, nothing like that. It is something you both may like very much. Again, this is not the time to read the letter as you both are preoccupied with Jack's funeral, and all your attention needs to be directed there. I would also want to thank you for helping Sophia with this unfortunate circumstance. She really is a very nice person and did not deserve this at all. But please wait until you get home to read it. Is it possible that after the funeral tomorrow you both could come and see me in the afternoon?"

"Well, I guess. We both have the entire day off from work. What time would be good?" asked Derrick.

"Would one or two o'clock work out? It probably will take a couple of hours to discuss the matter."

"I will say yes for now, but if for some reason Robyn can't make it, I will call you as soon as I can."

Mr. Watson wrote down his personal phone number and said, "If you cannot make it in tomorrow, please call me at this number anytime. I really need to get back to the office so I will see you tomorrow at 1pm unless I hear from you."

"Okay," said Derrick.

When Derrick got back to the parlor, he noticed that Steve Conti was there talking with Sophia. "Hi Derrick. Just having a few words with Sophia. She seems to be holding up pretty well."

"Glad you were able to visit. Who is running the Oasis? asked Derrick.

"I have Tom Patrick, our gaming pit boss, filling in for me. He does a good job and knows to call me if necessary. You know, I do a damn good job of running that casino and have things pretty much in control." Again, he noticed an arrogant tone. "Hey, meet my girlfriend, Sam Collins."

"Hi there Derrick, it is really Samantha but I like Sam," she said with a sexy smile. Now Sam is a very attractive, tan, mid to upper thirties, woman. She is wearing a black dress about 2-3 inches above the knee, with long flowing dark brown hair and heavy make up.

"It's nice to meet you," replied Derrick as Robyn looked on with a smirk on her face.

Steve added, "She also works as one of our dealers and is damn good at it. Derrick, I need to ask you something. Can we go over there in the back where there is no one arround?"

"Will this take long?"

"No just a minute or two."

Derrick told Robyn that he and Steve would be in the back of the parlor for just a few minutes and would be right back. Sam went over to a chair on the side wall and sat down crossing her well curved legs with six inch heels. She waited for Steve to come over.

"What's going on?" asked Derrick.

"The police called and said that since Jack died, this is now a murder investigation. I'm not to leave the area during the investigation. I believe they will be contacting you also. Were you in contact with Jack before he died?" Steve understood Jack's relationship with Derrick and was fishing for some information concerning the Lucky Oasis Casino.

"I have not seen Jack in about three weeks. Why do you ask?" Derrick said somewhat puzzled.

"Well I just thought that since you are such great friends and since Jack really does not have any family other than his sickly mother, you might know something about who is going to run the Oasis."

"Really, Steve. Today at Jack's funeral, you want to know who will run the Oasis?" Derrick said with firmness. He continued, "I can't believe this. For your information, NO, I do not know anything about that. Maybe Watson and Peters Law Firm does. This conversation is over!" "Sorry, just thought you might know something. Just be prepared when the police contact you." Derrick looked concerned saying, "Why will the police contact me?"

Steve offered, "Well, you are good friends. They probably will want to know who will be taking over the Lucky Oasis. I really don't know Derrick, but I would just be on guard if they do."

They both returned up front. Derrick went over to Robyn who was standing next to Sophia. "Steve came over and said, "Sam and I will be leaving now. I've got to get back to the Oasis. See you later." "I'm sure you will," said Derrick.

Robyn noticed some friction between the two and asked Derrick, "What's that all about?" Derrick told Robyn, "Forget about it, I will tell you later." Robyn also wanted to know what the lawyer wanted and again Derrick quietly said, "I'll tell you later."

Sophia's girl friends were still seated by her as the visitation came to a close. Derrick said to Sophia, "Ready to go home?"

"Yes" she said.

One of Sophia's friends said, "If you don't mind, I can take Sohpia home. We all live close by." "That would be okay. I will pick you up (looking at Sophia) tomorrow at 8:15 for the funeral." The funeral owner, Matthew Gordon, followed them out and said he would meet them at Saint Martin Church in the morning.

Chapter

3

THE CONDITIONAL INHERITANCE

Robyn barely closed the car door and said, "Okay, what the hell is going on? Tell me about what you and Steve talked about." Derrick started the car and drove out of the parking lot.

"You won't believe this, but Steve asked me if Jack said anything to me about who is going to own and run the Oasis."

"What? At Jack's funeral and he's only been gone for a few days!" exclaimed Robyn.

"Yea, the nerve of the son-of-a-bitch! I told him the same thing. He also thinks the police will want to talk to us."

"About what?!"

"Because we are good friends with Jack, and they may be looking for who will benefit from his death. Sounds like to me that Steve is worried that we may be Jack's beneficiary. Come to think about it, that brings me to what Al Watson, the lawyer, said and gave to me. "Here," reaching into his sport coat pocket and pulling out an envelope and giving it to Robyn. "Open this and read it out loud." Robyn opened the envelope and started reading. "Dear Mr. and Mrs. Derrick

Burns: It has been my privilege to represent Jack Capano and the Lucky Oasis Casino and Lodge for the past three years. Jack has set up receivership of the entire casino and lodge, with some restrictions, to his good friends Derrick and Robyn Burns, if so agreed, effectively upon his death.

"WHAT? JACKS IS OFFERING HIS CASINO TO US?!!" Derrick busted in.

"Hold on," continued Robyn, "There is a little more. For the privacy and protection of all, full details and procedures of this transaction will take place at the law office of Watson and Peters on the agreed upon date between both parties. Sincerely, Albert Watson, Attorney."

"Wholly fuck!" Derrick said not believing what he just heard. He pulled the car into a McDonald's and parked it to get his head around this. "Can you believe this, Jack's casino!" Now I understand why he insisted that I open the envelope at home and why he wanted to see us both tomorrow at 1pm."

"Tomorrow?" asked Robyn.

"Yea, he wanted to handle this as soon as possible and cleared that time for us. The funeral should be over by 10:30 or 11:00. I'm thinking Sophia would like to go out for brunch and that 1:00pm should be doable."

"I guess you're right. We need to find out all the details and what the restrictions are. Let's get home now so we can discuss this fully," Robin added.

The time was 9:15 when they got home. First thing, Derrick headed for the refrigerator and pulled out a Bud. Robyn also asked him to get her a Bud Light. Together they went over to the living room and sat in his and hers recliners. "This is fuckin unbelievable!" a stunned Robyn said and added, "I never ever thought Jack would die at this young age, let alone want us to run his casino. How much money do we need to put into this? Why did he set this up now? I mean, he only had the casino for three or four years. Isn't that right?"

"Yep," said Derrick as he gulped down his beer, and went to the refrigerator for another. "Want one?" he asked.

"Not just yet. How does this affect our jobs? How and the hell does this affect our jobs, Derrick?"

"I don't think we should think about abandoning our jobs just yet, Robyn. We need to get all the details first. Didn't the letter say if we so agreed? Also, the restrictions may not be feasible. Plus, how much money do we need to put up for this?

Maybe we could still run the Oasis and keep our jobs. Maybe. Maybe. Maybe, oh damn. We need to find out what profits the Oasis delivers. That way we could compare to what we earn now. It may make sense to actually pursue this. One of us may be able to keep our current job. We really don't know how to respond until we hear and see all the details. This much I know. Before we commit one way or another, we both have to be on board."

"Hell yes!" agreed Robyn. "Fuck it, why don't we just put this aside for now and go to bed. I need some passionate sex. Are you up to this?"

With his eyes wide open he stated, "We'll find out, won't we?"

Robyn's perfect naked body jumped on Derrick before he could pull his pants off. He fiercely pushed his pants legs off with his toes as she smothered her lips onto his. They French kissed passionately for several minutes. She moved her warm body on top of his kissing his chest as she moved down his body. She sat

up saying, "Don't make me wait, Derrick!" He grabbed her, flipping her over as he got on top. Pushing up and down, up and down feverishly for several minutes with sexual moans and sounds of pleasure. To climax together was just spine tingling joy! Derrick rolled over slowly panting in ecstasy. "Wooa, were we up to this?"

Robyn looking up at the ceiling and answered, "Fuckin a!" Then she kissed him and they both fell asleep.

They got to Saint Martin Church by 8:30 for the 9:00 funeral Mass. The open casket was right in front of the altar. Sophia sat in the first pew along with Derrick and Robyn waiting for the service to start while some visitors walked around the casket saying their good byes to Jack and wishing Sophia well.

Twenty two people showed up for the Mass and heard Derrick give the eulogy on Jack. He kept it short but zeroed in on how Jack cared about people's well being. Always treating all workers and players with fairness and respect. He will be missed by all who knew him.

When the Mass was over, Sophia holding onto Derrick on one side and Robyn the other followed behind the casket. It was being wheeled out of the church and down a short walkway to Saint Martin's Cemetery. This was real convenient having a cemetery on the same grounds as the church. An altar boy brought out a folding chair for Sophia at the grave site. Twenty people including Sophia's four friends gathered for the short readings and comments. She was glad it only took 20 minutes as Sophia was suffering with her arthritis. When the priest was finished, Derrick thanked him and asked if he would like to join them for brunch. He declined due to another appointment. Derrick invited Sophia's friends to join them for brunch, and they thought that was very thoughtful. They all agreed that the Omelet House was the best place for breakfast or lunch.

After brunch, Sophia was taken home by her friend. Derrick and Robyn had about a half hour before their 1pm meeting with attorney Albert Watson. The Side Bet Bar is right next to the Omelet House and just 5 minutes to the lawyer's office. He looked at her and she looked at him with a smile and both went in to have a quick drink.

They had three minutes to spare when they arrived at the lawyer's office. The receptionist looked up and said, "May I help you?"

"Yes, I am Derrick Burns, and this is my wife Robyn. We made arrangements to see Mr. Watson at 1pm."

"Oh yes, that is right." she said knowing they were expected. "Let me tell Mr. Watson you are here. Please have a seat." Instead of intercom contact the receptionist left her desk and walked down a hallway. It did not take her long and she reappeared and said, "Right this way, Mr. Watson is expecting you."

Derrick and Robyn followed the receptionist into an office, and they were greeted by Albert Watson. "Good morning and thanks for coming in on such short notice. Please take a seat here in front of my desk. Please call me Al—I'm not that formal and I like using first names. Before we start please help yourselves to some coffee on the counter, pointing to the back wall." Both Derrick and Robyn declined coffee and sat down in the two comfortable leather desk type chairs in front of his desk.

Al pulled out a file and said, "I am sure you have many questions after reading the letter I gave to you. Did you both read it?"

"Yes, we did and as you can imagine, we have a ton of questions. Is Jack selling us the casino or what does 'running' the casino mean?"

"Before you start asking me questions I need to ask you this. I know that your decision on this is predicated on knowing many factors and that would only make sense. However, after I give you all the details and it looks favorable and feasible, will you then consider conditional ownership? Or, have you already made up your minds at this time?"

Derrick glanced at Robyn, "Conditional ownership? What does THAT mean? We thought we were going to be asked to run the casino. It never crossed our minds to actually owning the casino. And no, we have not made up our minds," looking at her again for some type of approval. "But we are very interested in hearing all there is to hear." Robyn made a nod and grinned.

"That's what I needed to hear," said Al satisfied with the answer.

Al sat back in his chair looking at Derrick and Robyn while pulling out a sheet of paper that had his agenda on it. He started by saying "An application for ownership of the Lucky Oasis Casino needs to be submitted to the Nevada Gaming Commission for review, if you decide to pursue being the owners. Since you both already have a license issued by the Nevava Gaming Commission for your employment at the Starbrite Casino, the review should not take very long. A few weeks or a couple of months the most. In addition, the police visited me this morning and asked me a series of questions, including your involvement in Jack's casino. I needed to inform them that Jack has requested transfer of ownership to you both. The police have been informed about the details, but I believe they need to talk with you on this also. This will not hold up the appliction but may delay some approvals."

"Why are we being questioned?" asked Robyn.

"This is a murder investigation and since you are involved in obtaining Jack's casino, they will need to ask you questions. Don't worry, just answer their questions honestly. They need to review all those with connections to Jack and his property. This is very routine in order to rule out who may be suspects or not. If you need any help or advice from me, let me know."

Al had the application in hand in case the Burns wanted to go forth so it could be submitted that day. At that point Derrick asked, "The Lucky Oasis must be worth millions. How much money do we need to provide or are there backers involved?

What about our employment at the Starbrite?"

Al put down his agenda and looking at Derrick said, "I believe you would have to resign from the Starbite. Being the owner of a casino has many demands. You will need to be available at all times when contacted by the Commission. There are many regulations, reports and audits that are required routinely, and they are time consuming. The every day activity will take up a lot of your time. Robyn, on the other hand, could probably stay employed at the Starbrite, if she wanted to. This, I believe, will all be settled in the review of your application. As far as your investment, I will get into that later. However, at this time I would not quit your positions at the Starbrite. Wait until you hear back from the NGC on your license approval."

Al added that since his law firm represented the Lucky Oasis and Jack himself, we have a good deal of knowledge about the entire operation. Here is some history about the Lucky Oasis. It is the last casino of two or three others just north of the town Jean on I-15. Most people traveling on this Interstate are from California going to Las Vegas. It is a highly competitive area with some casinos in the area going bankrupt or changing names often. The main reason for stopping at these casino's is for gas or a quick bite to eat. The Lucky Oasis Casino has been in operation nearly twelve years with three different owners. Jack worked at the Oasis with his father, Tony Capano, who bought it from Bill Stokey. Bill was the original owner, who died from a heart attack just about eight years ago. When Jacks's father died slipping on a wet floor, breaking his leg and getting a blood clot, Jack was devastated. He loved his dad very much and learned the casino business from him. Now Jack only had his mother left as family. As you can see, a new owner about every four years has some wondering if the casino is cursed. Not likely. Lucky Oasis continues to produce good profits month after month during Jack's ownership. Last year it profited two hundred, five thousand dollars. That is an excellent profit considering this is just a small off beat type of a casino. Mostly locals and West Coast travelers patronize it. Jack really increased its busines and profits when he went all out and promoted live country-western entertainment on Friday and Saturday nights. The lounge next to the cafe has a stage with a dance floor and this really brought in the crowds. The locals have many venues to choose from all around the Vegas area, but the Lucky Oasis is one of their favorites. "Still want me to go on?" asked Al.

Robyn answered, "YES! By all means! Doesn't this sound interesting, Derrick?"

"Yea, I think it does. I am a little concerned about how much money we are expected to come up with. I am concerned about that cursed thing and being questioned by the police. However, I liked the amount of profit that place delivered. I did not think those little casinos out there did that kind of business."

"The part about it being cursed--I believe it stems from some employee saying that it was because of the number of ownership deaths; nothing more than coincidence probably. Steve Conti would know more about this, if you need to follow up. You know Steve, don't you?" They both said, "Yes," so Al went on.

"Your investment would be a very modest seven thousand dollars mainly to cover my time and costs associated with the handling of the applications, title work, regulations and all the documents needed to complete this transaction. In other words, Jack is not selling you his casino but rather offering it to you with certain conditions. When those conditions have been met fully, then the casino complex will be completely yours to do with what you want," finished Al. Robyn looked a little perplexed asking, "What conditions?"

Al leaned forward a bit holding another sheet of paper saying, "Jack kept his casino profitable not only for his benefit and his workers but also for his mom. Twenty five percent of the profits needs to be set aside and deposited into his mother's checking account about every three months. That amounted to fifty one thousand dollars to his mother last year. That is one of the requirements and needs to be made as long as she is alive. In addition, since his mother has no one left in her family, he is asking you to look over her affairs along with my law firm. Also, in order to keep the casino operating in rough times (like when we went through that pandemic a couple of years ago), another twenty five percent needs to be taken from the profits and placed in the casino's 'special opperating fund.' Those funds can only be used when the business does not deliver enough profits to pay bills, taxes, repairs and payroll. It cannot be used to add any improvements, new ideas or other activity that could wait until profits returned to manageable means. Right now that special casino fund has one hundred, twenty two thousand dollars in it. That fund is also part of the conditional ownership. So, that means that one hundred, two thousand dollars was removed from last years profits leaving Jack with one hundred three thousand dollars." Al looked at both Derrick and Robyn and said, "Would that be enough for you to live on?"

"Well, said Derrick, Robyn and I cleared a little more than that last year at the Starbrite. So, yes, I guess that would work out. But what about down years?"

"That is what the special casino account is there for. Call it a rainy day account or emergency account or whatever. Hopefully you can put money into it every year and not have to use it. But when you do, it's there," answered Al. "Listen, there is no guarantee in life. We take chances every day. But I say this, reviewing the Oasis books for not only Jack's time but his father's time, the Oasis was profiting ninety six thousand dollars yearly for the owner, on average. That's eight years on average, except the year of the pandemic when everyone suffered.

"Yes I know," said Derrick. "My hours were cut in half, and Robyn was actually laid off for ten months."

"There you go," Al said.

Steve Conti called me this morning," as Al continued, "saying he was contacted again by the police with just some more questions. He then asked me what was going to happen to the Lucky Oasis due to Jack's death and if he is eligible to purchase the casino. What I said to him is that everything at this time is in limbo. His law firm would be handling all the legal matters and until that is resolved, there will be no comment. However, I am sure you know that Steve had the authority to handle all activity concerning the Oasis in the absence of Jack. So right now we have designated Steve temporary manager answering to me. No major changes can be made, and operation of the casino must continue as it is currently set up. He has proven, in the past, to handle matters fairly well and is an excellent maintenance guy that takes care of whatever needs fixing. He is not that outgoing, or should I say, as personable as Jack was but gets the job done.

One thing about Steve, that Jack mentioned to me several months ago, was he thought he was acting like he was the owner. He could not really pinpoint the reason how he felt, but just the way Steve was saying and doing things made him uncomfortable. I think if you actually take over, you would need to observe and watch Steve closely. That is if you, in fact, keep him on. And based on what has been said, all the workers there are very good employees. It is my belief they would want to continue working in their jobs even with new owners."

"Well, what do you think about this now?"

"Seriously, I am at a loss for words," said Derrick shaking his head.

"Absolutely unbelievable!" countered Robyn.

"Maybe you both should take a day or two to discuss and think this over before making any decisions," offered Al.

Derrick turned to Robyn and said, "This is a BIG deal! Do you think we should wait and talk this out?"

Robyn thought for a moment then said, "From what has been discussed, I feel pretty much like this is a once in a life time opportunity. We could sign the application to be conditional owners, since that apparently will take the longest to get approved, and ask Al not to mail it in until tomorrow. If we decide not to go forward with this, we can call him in the morning and tell him to tear it up," offered Robyn.

"Wow! Sounds like you really want this," replied Derrick.

"Don't you?" Not letting him answer she went on. "Look, if we get approved as owners of the Oasis and for some reason we cannot make a go of it, screw it. We can then ask Al to find different owners. Right, Al? He nodded yes. "Are we not getting one hundred twenty two thousands dollars to start with?" inquired Robyn.

"Well that is correct, Robyn, but remember that is for rainy days."

"Signing the Commissions application would make sense, Al said. There are a lot of details that need to be answered, and in this way, it avoid's having you make another trip back here. Even if I sent it into the NGC and you changed your minds, you could cancel. In fact, you could even cancel after being approved."

Robyn raised her hands up and said, "That settles it for me. I say we make a stab at this. How about it, honey?"

"She only calls me honey when she wants something," Derrick said looking at Al. "Fine, let's sign the app and get this thing started."

"In my observation," stated Al, I believe you both have the casino experience and a good personality with a desire to achieve. Plus, you are both young enough that if this does not work out, you could get out with minimum outlay of funds and start over. One more thing. When approved, there is the matter of ownership title and the banking accounts we need to get transferred. Do not worry, as I will get all the details in order and contact you so you will have ample time to get your affairs in order. Please DO NOT discuss this with anyone or even go to the Oasis to ask any questions, especially to Steve. If you want to go there to gamble and have some drinks, fine, but refrain from anything related to ownership." They both understood what Al was saying.

Chapter

4

NEW OWNERS

It was not like they thought and talked about owning a casino every moment of every non-work day of free time they had. When they were together at home, they did discuss the advantages and disadvantages of being owners but not to the level that it drove them nuts. The anticipation of waiting to see if they even had a chance was somewhat unnerving. So when they received a letter from the Nevada Gaming Commision, nearly four weeks later that they were approved, the anxiety level was lifted as great relief. They celebrated sort of with the idea that their lives were now about to change.

The letter stated to contact the Law Office of Watson and Peters to prepare and finalize details for title, tax accounts, bank accounts and all the details of Nevada's legal requirements and policies in performing and conducting casino ownership responsibilities. They thought Al Watson was to contact them on the approval so they were surprised to get this letter. Since it was after 5 pm Tuesday, they decided to call Al the next morning. Derrick called Al from work on his break at around 10:10am and made arrangements for a meeting next Monday morning at ten. He contacted Robyn saying she needed to get Monday off. "If anyone asks why, just say we have a legal matter to get settled," he said.

Robyn was already in the pool with a beer in hand when Derrick waltzed in. He knew she was in the pool so he undressed, put on his swimsuit, got a beer and went out jumping into the pool holding his beer up. They both pressed their bodies together in hugs and kisses. "So, we are going to be casino owners!"

"Guess so... conditional owners," she said with a smile. "Do you really want to go out for dinner or would you like to stay home, order a pizza, stay in our swimsuits, drink beer and have sex?"

"Sounds good to me. Why do we need swimsuits?"

After getting out of the pool, Derrick pulled Robyn's wet body to his wet body and hugging her said, "I love you to death, Robyn." Then he passionately kissed her. "Back at you more!" she answered. "You after something?" Feeling his man tool getting rock hard."

"Maybe. But first I think we need to go over the pros and cons of this adventure we are heading into." He went on, "Just wanting to make sure we both understand what we are getting ourselves into. Both of us need to be one hundred percent in agreement."

Robyn understood what he was saying. Knowing how Derrick would go over and over issues before he would actually do something said, "Again Derrick? We have gone over this quite a bit the last four weeks. Like I said before, if you have any fucking doubts at all, let's just say to Al we are not ready and dump this."

"You have any doubts? Are you ready to go?" he asked.

"NO! YES! Shit! I believe there will always be doubts, Derrick. But how many times are we going to go over and over this opportunity before we say yes or no. I am ready to give this a shot. But if you are not ready then I say, fuck it, and let us forget about the whole damn thing! I will support you if you do not want to move on with this."

"Okay, okay I agree. Sorry I am such a fucking stick in the mud. You are right, we should take this opportunity and try to make something of it."

"Then let's put this aside and out of our minds until we meet with Al next Monday," proclaimed Robyn. "How about ordering the damn pizza? I'm hungry!"

The police contacted the Burns on Saturday saying the suspects that killed Jack have been found, and they were no longer involved. This was, in a way, welcome news. Now they just needed to wait two more days for their Monday meeting with Al.

Getting up early Monday was not difficult. They were eager for their meeting with lawyer Al. They dressed casually. Robyn put on blue skin tight jeans and a black sleeveless v-neckline blouse. Derrick wore blue jeans and a blue-green tropical short sleeve shirt. They decided to go out for breakfast on their way to their meeting with Al.

Walking in, the receptionist remembers them and asked them to take a seat. Using the intercom she announced, "The Burns have arrived." "Send them right in," he said.

"Well, are you ready to be business owners of a casino?" Al asked.

"I believe we are," Derrick firmly answered as he glanced at Robyn.

"I'm NOT! Blasted Robyn. He's been nothing but a royal pain in the ass!" Robyn said pointing to Derrick.

"WHAT?" he shouted.

"Only kidding. Just wanted to get back at you, dear," she said smiling.

"Sounds like you both had an exciting time discussing all this the past few weeks," jumped in Al.

"Yes, to say the least," smiled Robyn.

Al informed them, "The reason you received approval notification from the Nevada Gaming Commission is that they are required to send out replies to all parties involved on license applications. This is something I neglected to mention to you at our last meeting. Sorry about that. But now you know that you are set to go and can take the conditional title of Lucky Oasis Casino and Lodge." He asked them again if they were prepared to move forward. Both agreed.

Al then brought out a bunch of documents and said, "Let the signing begin."

With the signing and explaining of each document it took nearly ninety minutes. After that, they all took a break for coffee and donuts. When they returned to Al's desk he said, "All these documents including the title work will take several days to a couple of weeks to get completed. I will fast track them as best as I can. In the meantime, you should make plans about your current employment at the Starbrite."

Derrick said, "Yes, Robyn and I have talked about this until we were blue in the face. We finally decided that I would hand in my resignation and she would continue at the Starbrite helping me out on the weekends."

Robyn added, "I feel like it would be a good idea for me to stay employed until we have a better understanding of how things turn out. Also, I can add Derrick to my health care coverage on the family plan and not to the Lucky Oasis plan."

"That sounds like a sensible way to start out," mentioned Al.

"We have finished the 'paper work' part of this adventure. Now you can make plans on how you will be carrying out the managing part. I think this might be a good time to contact Steve and let him know that you will be taking over operations. Even though you do not have the final documents in hand, you will be operating the Oasis under my guidance until they are received."

"I will also contact Steve today to let him know what is taking place. I will mention to him that the reason we could not entertain his purchasing the Oasis was due to Jack's request for his friends, the Burns, to manage his casino. I believe you know how to calmly relay this to Steve. He can be of great value and help in your transformation, or maybe not. If handled properly, I think Steve will understand and be an asset."

"Do you have any questions?" asked Al.

"So, we can start running the Lucky Oasis right now?" asked Robyn.

"Yes," he said. "Along with Watson and Peters Law Firm for guidance and direction. So you can jump right in anytime. Any changes in operation or anytime you need some advice, please call us. Here is my cell number. Call me after hours when you need some information of importance that cannot wait until daytime. Have you been in contact with Sophia lately?"

"Yes. We called and stopped over a couple of times while waiting for the approval," said Derrick.

"Great! I am glad you did. Remember, she has no one else in her family to take care of her needs. She, and I, appreciate you taking this on. It should pay off in big dividends to you both."

"Thanks for all your help with this Al," said Derrick. "I think Robyn and I will head over to the Lucky Oasis to talk with Steve. Maybe we'll take him out to lunch feel him out and stuff. Again, thanks." They left the law firm, got into his Forester and headed out to the Lucky Oasis.

Chapter 5

THE CURSES

Derrick and Robyn were very excited about their opportunity to run a casino. They wanted to go out and celebrate but also wanted to remain calm and relaxed when they visited Steve. "How do you think Steve is going to accept this?" asked Robyn.

"Not sure, Robyn."

"Do you think we should give him a head's up call?"

"Naw. Al might have already called him. Let's just go there and see if he wants to go to lunch or something." They arrived at the Lucky Oasis just after 1pm.

It is Monday and the parking lot had about ten parked vehicles indicating promising business. The marquee outside is not big but a good size for this type of off beat casino. The top had Lucky Oasis with neon green for Lucky and neon gold for Oasis. It also has a color LED message display. On it said 'Welcome' on top and 'County and Western' nights Friday & Saturday featuring "Silver Spurs."

The Burns walked in through the front door and looked for Steve. Not seeing him they walked over to the cashier while noticing there were three blackjack players and several players at the slots. They asked the cashier where Steve was. She asked them who they were and they said friends of his. She paged Steve, and he told her to send them upstairs to the office.

Steve emerged from the counting room and seeing Derrick and Robyn walking into the office greeted them with, "Look who's here. The new owners of the Lucky Oasis."

Derrick smiled saying, "So Al called you? We just came from his office. Have you been to lunch yet?"

"Actually no. I have been busy trying to get the counting room in order after getting the news from Al," informed Steve.

"Why don't we go somewhere so we can relax, have lunch and discuss what's going on," suggested Derrick.

Steve offered, "We can have lunch here in our Eatery. We have great hamburgers, grilled chicken breast and things like that."

"That sounds great, and we know the food is good here," said Robyn. Steve commented on how good Robyn looked and led the way to the Eatery.

The Eatery was a small place opposite the casino next to the stairs going up to the office. There are four tables and three booths to hold twenty eight diners. The busiest time for The Eatery was 11am until 2pm. Many travelers from California would stop there for lunch before heading to their Vegas destination. This day it was not very busy. Just six people were eating. The limited menu was posted on the wall featuring reasonably priced popular sandwich type meals. Steve selected a cheeseburger, Derrick ordered the Italian beef and Robyn a grilled chicken breast. Derrick tried to pay for lunch but Steve said "Why would you guys pay; you own the place. "Not exactly correct, Steve. But we'll get into that shortly," offered Derrick.

As they stood waiting for their food, both Derrick and Robyn looked around to see the decor that had large colored framed photos of many Las Vegas casinos. In between the photos were colored cardboard dice, cards and wheels depicting gaming excitement.

This decor has been there for a long time and still looked fairly good. The same gal that took their order delivered them. They sat at the end booth.

Derrick took a bite out of his Italian beef and said, "This is not bad." "The chicken breast is just right for me," added Robyn.

"We get very little complaints about the food here," stated Steve.

Derrick was looking for a gentle way to bring up the ownership change when he said, "You know Steve, Robyn and I were very much surprised and shocked when we found out about what Jack had in mind with this casino. We never dreamed or even thought about something like this. We also knew from the lawyer that you have been Jack's right hand man. You are very good at seeing that things get done here."

"Yea, that didn't seem to do me any good in trying to get ownership of this place."

Derrick looked Steve into the eye saying, " We almost turned down the offer of taking on the Oasis, Steve. Jack set up a 'conditional ownership' that requires us to look after his mom, and set aside twenty five percent of the profits for her benefit, so long as she is alive. Jack was our best friend. We loved and respected him and his mom, and since we did not have to shell out a large sum of money, we accepted the conditions. It is more like Robyn and I are managing Jack's casino."

"Wholly shit!" shouted Steve and continued, "One quarter of the busines to his mom! Glad it was you and not me. Besides, I was going to have a hard time getting the backing that I would need. Even if I did get it, the investors would never accept those terms. You think you guys are going to make it on seventy five percent of the profits?"

"We hope so," answered Derrick.

"I will be offering my resignation to the Starbrite so I can be here as much as possible. Robyn plans on staying employed at the Starbrite and helping here when she can. We also need to keep Al informed weekly on conditions, suggestions and any changes we want to make. We also must fill out and submit the financial report to NGC with a copy to Al. Yes, we do not have to pay a huge sum of money for the Oasis, but we are risking a lot by taking on this venture."

Both Derrick and Robyn were glad to hear Steve say he would have had a difficult time securing backing and that he would never agree to giving up twenty five percent of the profits. "Now that we understand the roles we are in, Robyn and I would like you to stay on to be our manager when we cannot be here. Much like what you are doing now."

"Well, I probably would consider that Derrick. Just need to know what to expect as to compensation and benefits."

Derrick said, "Your current salary and benefits will continue until we get the final documents and word from Al that everything is in order. Robyn and I will be managing this place, but with the direction from Al. When it is official, we will be able to discuss all your concerns and conditions at that time." Steve nodded in agreement.

"How about this curse thing the lawyer mentioned?" Robyn asked.

"Let's get out of The Eatery and I'll tell you about that as we inspect the place.

How about a drink first?" suggested Steve. Adjacent to The Eatery is the Oasis Lounge. They all went in and Steve called Don over, the afternoon bartender.

Steve was hesitant getting a drink until Derrick said it was okay. All three took a Bud Light and sat down in the dimly lit lounge. Many tables and stand up drink tables were spread neatly about. The stage was a good size for an off beat bar.

Steve said, "On Friday and Saturday nights this place is packed. A good part of our income is derived from this lounge."

As they relaxed in the lounge Steve addressed how the curse started. "Bill Stokey had this place built about twelve years ago. During the final stages of construction, a worker slipped on some board or something falling, hitting his head and died on April 4 at 4pm. His wife was furious saying that the workers were careless and pledged a curse on the Lucky Oasis. Now four years later Bill died of a heart attack on April 4 around 4pm. When the Stokey family put it up for sale, Tony Capano, Jack's dad, bought the casino. That is when I came aboard as Tony's maintenance man. Jack also joined up and learned from his dad how to manage a casino. Four years later on April 3 it just finished raining outside and the tile floor was wet when Tony slipped, breaking his leg. He then got a blood clot and died the next day on April 4 at 4pm. Jack inherited the Oasis and was shot this past August 22nd and rushed to the hospital. He died on August 24th at 4pm. That resulted in four persons (owners) dying in four year increments, on April 4 or August 24, at around 4pm at this casino. Some suggest that the place may be cursed.

I do not understand the August 24 versus April thing. Maybe the month's first letter starting with an 'A' has some meaning to it. I don't really know. Still, the time was 4pm when Jack died."

"So this is why you believe the casino is cursed?" asked Robyn.

"Yaaa, but not just because of the same month and time of four deaths," answered Steve. "There is this loud bell that rings once every minute on April 4 at 4pm and stops twenty minutes later. It is like a loud dull death bell sound. It comes through our sound system and we cannot get it to stop. Every once in a while we are asked what does that bell mean, and we say were working on a new promotion. It only happens on April 4$^{th.}$ Then there is the full moon experience. Every full moon at midnight the casino lights flicker then go on and flicker again and go on for about twenty minutes. I have tried everything including having an electrician test all circuits, outlets and cannot find anything wrong. Also on Halloween night from 4pm to midnight our sound system that pipes music into the casino plays only weird loud spooky organ music. We cannot change channels or even turn the system off. Again, we cannot find any way to correct this. I really don't mind the spooky organ music since it's only on

Halloween anyway. Actually none of these so-called curses are a big deal as they occur so infrequently."

Derrick seemed somewhat troubled saying, "Looks to me like we need to be mostly concerned about the death part every four years."

"Yeah, maybe it is all a coincidence, hopefully. But it is four owners in four year increments, on certain months, at about 4pm that have died here," stated Steve.

"Has anyone tried to contact the wife of the construction worker that died from this so-called curse of hers?" asked Robyn.

"Good point, Robyn. I do not believe anyone has. I will look into it."

Robyn upset with this added, "Now I'm fucking concerned. This does not seem like someting we can just brush off."

Derrick glanced at Robyn saying, "What do you suppose we do about it now?

Hang it up? Call it quits?"

"What I am saying, Derrick, is what if it is your damn turn in four years!"

Getting a little pissed off he said, "So you actually think this is a REAL curse and that four years from now I, you, or both of us will die from something?"

Robyn barked, "Four fucking deaths, every four fucking years on April 4 at 4pm, Derrick, might not be just a damn fucking coincidence!"

"Okay, okay, Robyn, let me say this. We continue with this and in three and one- half years from now if we still have bells ringing on April 4 at 4pm, flickering lights on full moons, spooky organ music on Halloween nights, then we just call the lawyer and tell him we are done with this fucking place. Sound good?"

"HELL YES! Make it three years after Halloween." she firmly said.

Now Steve was just sitting quitely observing the back and forth of the two of them when he jumped in, "You guys can really get it on. Again, I will try and locate Bill's wife and see if we can get to talk with her. But I think what you said about seeing how things play out in three and one-half years, sounds sensible to me."

"Three years after this Halloween!" snapped Robyn.

"Alright, said Steve. Why don't we go and look over the place to see what's what."

"Agreed," said Derrick.

"I want a whiskey sour to go," Robyn said firmly. Steve and Derrick smiled, got her the whiskey sour and off they all went to review the property.

Chapter 6

PROPERTY REVIEW

The Oasis Lounge is separated from the casino area with a half wall that has a ledge for those standing outside to place their drinks on top. This was used for overflow crowds that could not get inside or gaming people to stop by and listen briefly to the bands. Derrick, Robyn and Steve walked out of the open doorway into the casino area. All types of slots were lined up opposite the lounge. This set up allowed for the table games to be somewhat away from the direct band sounds. Table game players could still hear the band music but not have the direct sound by being in front of the lounge. While Derrick and Robyn visited the Lucky Oasis several times to see Jack and do some gaming, they never came in on Friday or Saturday nights.

Derrick seemed pleased with the slot set up saying, "This took a lot of thought; it looks real good."

"Thanks," Steve said proudly. "This whole arrangement was my idea, and Jack also liked it."

Robyn said, "I like how there is enough room between the slots for handicap players to move around. Have you ever had any slot tournaments or promotions?"

"Not really, Robyn," replied Steve. "We get a lot of older local people who come here mainly during the day. They like this casino because of the quiet and no hustle-bustle like in Vegas. They like our slot and video poker assortment and room between them as many use walkers and such. As for tournaments and promotions, Jack and I felt like it would not produce much more following." They all headed over to the table games area. There is only one pit with four blackjack tables, two side by side and back to back, with a 3-card poker table at one end forming the pit. There's one roulette table against the wall opposite the blackjack. Only one blackjack table was open with three players. Roulette was open, but the dealer sat behind it waiting for players as she read a book. Dealer's in Vegas could not do this. They must stand at their table waiting for players. But here, it was more relaxed and accepted. As Derrick observed the table game set up he asked, "Why is the roulette against the wall?" Steve said, "To have the dealer's back against the wall."

Derrick did not concur and offered, "Taking the rouette and putting it at the other end of the blackjack pit would seal off the pit itself. That would prevent access to the pit except for dealers. That would open up more room for slots against the wall."

Steve remarked, "Jack and I tried to keep the card game activity together and never thought about capping the other end of the pit with roulette. Now that you mentioned it, I think that would be a good idea."

Robyn strolled over to the lodge's small registration counter on the other side of the steps going to the office. No one was present and if you wanted to register for a room, there was a bell with a little sign that said 'press bell to register.' Robyn went behind the counter when Steve and Derrick appeared. Steve pointed out that rarely does anyone come to the Oasis to stay except couples out for an evening fling...or if one had too much to drink. "What happens when someone presses the bell?" asked Robyn.

"The manager on duty or the supervisor of gaming during weekdays would come over to assist," Steve explained. "Again, not very often do we have anyone that wants a room during the week. Now on Friday and Saturday nights, in the casino area only, we have a part time drink waitress, Connie, that can also register guests. This is usually for those who stayed until closing and prefer not to drive."

Steve led them to the lodge rooms through the hallway opening door next to the registration counter. An outside door offered entrance to the hallway on both sides. This allowed those staying to enter the front rooms or as a side entrance to the casino. There are ten rooms on both sides of the hallway. At the end of the hallway was another door.

The first two rooms on the north side of the hallway were never rented. These rooms were used only by Jack. One was his private office and the other was for him to relax or sleep in. Steve explained all rooms were virtually the same in size and set up. They were kept clean by the same person, Rosemary Vargas. She cleaned the entire casino complex Sunday through Thursday. A part time gal, Carmen Faria, worked on Friday and Saturday. Since the casino closed from three to seven in the morning every day for cleaning, all doors were locked including the guest room hallway door to the casino. Derrick and Robyn never stayed here so they viewed one of the rooms. It was small but clean; typical motel type room with king bed, desk, chair, tv and phone. The ten rooms on the north side were smoking, and the ten rooms on the south side were non-smoking. After reviewing the lodge, they all went up to the office to look at the counting room.

Steve opened the counting room door inside the office. They observed a coin counting machine, bill counting machine, stacks of rolled gaming chips on an oversized rectangle table in the middle of the room. A large floor safe stood against the wall. A small freight elevator was next to the safe. Everything seemed neatly placed in order. Derrick asked, "Who do we have as the accountant or money counter?"

"Jerry Duncan does all the counting and book work. He has been here since Tony was the owner and is very good at what he does. He handles all of the required filings and financial reports that need to be submitted," informed Steve. "I will need to meet with Jerry very soon, Steve. What days and hours does he work?" Steve replied, "Jerry works Monday, Wenesday and Friday from 8am to 5pm."

"Well Steve, Robyn and I need to get home. It has been a long day. We thank you for your time, showing us around and all your input."

My pleasure Derrick," said Steve. "I will be in contact with you soon. I plan on being here some evenings and on the weekends until I leave the Starbrite. In the meantime, please keep the place afloat and call me or Robyn on any matters you think we should know about."

"I will Derrick. Keep safe and well."

Chapter 7

STAFF MEEETING

During the drive home Derrick said, "You were not talking a lot except for the curse thing. You alright with this set up?"

Robyn stared straight ahead saying, "Derrick, I think Jack's casino is a very nice place with a lot of potential. I am just terribly concerned about how four guys died, four years apart and at the same time at that casino. How can that *not* be a fucking curse?"

"I am concered too, Robyn. Let's hope Steve can locate the phone number of that wife that put this so-called curse on. I would like to contact her, if she is still alive."

"What if she is? Do you think she would actually lift that fucking curse?"

"I don't know, Robyn. But if she is alive, I damn well want to contact her and see what we can do about it. If that fails, we just do what we said. Three years from this Halloween we let this damn thing go and turn it all back to the law firm of Watson and Peters.

Today marked the end of Derrick's two week notice. Starbrite Casino hated to lose Derrick after five years of excellent service. His boss, Gus, wished him well and if things did not work out for him that he would always be welcomed back. He was well liked and since it was Friday, four of his co-workers, along with Robyn, went out for a few drinks wishing him the best. Derrick and Robyn thought about going over to the Lucky Oasis but decided to wait until tomorrow. They were both tired and knew they would be there all day on Saturday and would need a good night's sleep.

Getting up late, on this Saturday, Robyn made bacon and eggs with toast for breakfast. After breakfast, they both headed out to the Lucky Oasis to spend the entire day there. Derrick called Steve in advance to set up a short meeting with all the weekend staff at 1pm. He also called Sophia and told her that whatever Jack had set up for her from the Oasis, he and Robyn would see to it that it would continue.

They would plan on seeing her as soon as they were able to get all their affairs in order.

It was about ten minutes before one when Derrick and Robyn entered the Lucky Oasis and were greeted by Steve. "Where do you want to meet?"

"How about in the lounge?" offered Derrick.

"Perfect," said Steve. He used the PA system to call all workers to the lounge.

As they headed to the lounge Robyn asked Steve, "Did you find out anything about that witch who put the curse on the Oasis?" "Let's talk about that after the meeting," Steve said.

"How was last night?" asked Derrick.

"We had a good crowd. There weren't as many as usual but still decent."

There were only two people playing the slots. So the entire staff was available for the meeting. Derrick opened the meeting saying, "Good afternoon. My name is Derrick Burns, and this is my wife Robyn. We will keep this meeting very short. Jack was my best friend; and when he passed, he wanted his casino to continue like he set it up. So he named just one as custodians, so to speak. We will be managing the Lucky Oasis for Jack, and we look forward to working with all of you. Right now there will be very little changes as we observe the routine and the procedures that are in place. Does anyone have any questions?"

The weekend cleaning gal, Carmen Faris asked, "Will we still stay open for twenty hours closing at 3am and reopening at 7am?"

"Yes," Derick said and continued "Again, very little will be changed right away. Your compensation and any benefits and hours will all stay the same for now. Please feel free to see me or Robyn anytime you have a question or a problem. Also, Steve here, will be staying on and will be the manager on duty when Robyn and I cannot be here."

Robyn added, "We want everyone to know that we appreciate what you do and value your contribution to the Lucky Oasis. Please offer any suggestions or ideas you may have. We have some ideas planned, but we need your input so we can continue in the spirit of Jack, not only making the Lucky Oasis profitable, but a fun place to work."

Steve standing off to the side said, "I have known Derrick and Robyn for a long time, and I am sure you all will enjoy working for them."

"Any more questions or comments?" asked Derrick.

The day bartender on Saturday and Sundays, Bob, asked, "Are you just the managers or the owners?"

"Good question. It is a little complicated for us to go into details at this time. For now, we will just be managing the Lucky Oasis with the guidance Jack left us. Any other questions? Good. Thank you. Have a great fun day, and we will look forward to our working relationships."

Steve, Derrick and Robyn stopped at the Eatery, picked up coffee, and went up to the office. "I think that meeting settled any anxiety the staff may have had about new ownership," said Steve.

"I think so for now," mentioned Robyn. "Now we need to meet the weekend night crew. Let's meet in the lounge again around five thirty."

"Hopefully we can discuss our meet and greet in time before the shift changes," offered Derrick.

In the office Robyn said, "How about that bitch and her curse, Steve?"

Steve motioned Derrick to sit in the desk chair, Robyn sat in a cushioned chair in the corner, and Steve walked behind Derrick. He pulled out a file from the middle drawer giving it to Robyn and said, "Here, this is what I could find about that woman and her curse." The file showed her name was Wendy Stokey, living in Desert Inn Estates, city of Las Vegas. Steve said, "I called her, and she did not want to discuss her curse and hung up on me."

"Looks like we need to make a person to person visit to this bitch," snapped Robyn.

"You're probably right, Robyn. But we need to approach her cautiously and gently if we are going to have any chance to get this resolved," offered Derrick. Then he added, "Remember, she lost her husband building this place. Maybe we should make a visit to her next Monday morning and tell her, nicely, that we are the new owners and if we can do something to compensate her loss." "Shit, I doubt that would work," said Steve.

Robyn added, "I work on Monday."

"Maybe I should just visit her myself. I need to at least try and see if we can get this corrected. I would like to review the books now and how and when we make pick ups and stuff like that."

It was nearly noon when all three reviewed the operating books, discussed the timing of picking up the cash boxes, and when the daily report sheets were made. Basically, how everyone performed their duties each day. They also went through the number of personnel on hand and if additional workers were needed. This also included compensation, pay schedules and all working procedures for each area of operation. This was very informative and time consuming and before they knew it, time was approaching their evening meeting.

The evening meeting had more staff members as it was Saturday Country and Western night. Samantha (Sam) Conti, Steve's girlfriend, arrived first. Wearing tight full length jeans with a red velvet V-Neck, short sleeve blouse exposing some cleavage. With long black hair and tons of makeup, she looked like a movie star.

Steve asked her to wait at the employee entrance and direct everyone to the lounge for a brief meeting.

All night shift employees met in the lounge at 5:30. Derrick and Robyn went through the meeting in fifteen minutes. Everyone seemed to be on board with the change over, and were apparently ready to see how it all played out.

After the meeting Derrick noticed that four of the dealers for blackjack were all sexy, good looking girls dressed in jeans with low cut tops. The Lucky Oasis did not have uniforms so this dress was appropriate for Country and Western nights. He and Robyn went around to visit each dealer as they started their shifts. Robyn with a smirky smile told Derrick, "Better lay your hands off Sam." He just rolled his eyes. All games were opened, as was the case on Friday and Saturday nights.

Now all they needed was a good turnout.

The popular band, Silver Spurs, was getting set up on the stage in the lounge. People were filing in even before seven so as to get good seats. The band did not even start until nine. Some even ordered from the Eatery. There were several people playing table games and slots. This was shaping up to indicate another packed Saturday night at the Lucky Oasis. Steve took Derrick and Robyn over to meet the band members. He mentioned that Derrick would pay them at closing. Steve said it was customary to offer all band members free food and anything they wanted to drink. This was necessarry as the bands they brought in were popular top line groups that opened many times for the big acts in the Las Vegas area. These bands, when they had open dates, enjoyed playing at the Oasis Lounge. Steve asked Derrick if he and Robyn were okay with handling the rest of the night. He wanted to leave so he could come in Sunday morning at 7 am to open up. They both agreed and thought this would be a real challenge for getting their feet wet. Steve said to call him if needed, and he left.

Packed was an understatement. At nine thirty the Burns were simply amazed seeing the gaming tables filled and the Oasis Lounge jammed with the crowd over flow standing outside against the railings. Silver Spurs were playing Country Rock, and the atmosphere was filled with fun. People were having a good time all over the place. Derrick noticed a uniformed police officer by the lounge entrance. He went over to talk with him. Derrick introduced himself and Robyn. He asked if they ever have any problems at the Oasis. "Rarely," he answered. "Mostly locals patronize here, and they respect the property as a place they can go to without facing undesirables. I am a retired Vegas cop and enjoy working here," he said. They both were pleased hearing that and offered the officer some coffee or water, which he accepted.

Derrick went over to the gaming tables to help out. Robyn went to the lounge and saw they needed help serving drinks. She was glad they had two bartenders. If every Friday and Saturday night was like this, it was no wonder the Lucky Oasis was so profitable.

At closing, Derrick and Robyn were exhausted. They just spent sixteen hours working at the Lucky Oasis. Everyone was now gone except Tom, the pit supervisor, and the police officer. All the cash boxes had to be transferred to the counting room upstairs before they could leave. They let the officer go after locking all the doors. Tom, Derrick and Robyn took the cash boxes on a cart to the freight elevator. Then up to the counting room. They just left them on the huge center table for counting on Sunday. Robyn wrote a note to Steve that the cash boxes were not counted and to set up new boxes for the day. They then left.

Chapter

8

MEETING THE WITCH

After getting home around 4 am, Derrick and Robyn did not get up until eleven on Sunday morning. They both crawled out of bed looking at each other thinking, WOW! What a night! Derrick strolled into the shower first. Robyn made coffee, and put the dirty clothes in the washer. She told Derrick that the coffee was made as he left the shower. Derrick dressed while Robyn showered. They both were moving in slow motion.

As they sat drinking coffee, Robyn asked, "Do you want breakfast?" "Yep, I do." "Then, why don't you fuckin make it?" "Oh Robyn, we are both tired. Why don't we just sit and drink coffee for a bit. Let's relax and talk about last night's packed house. Shit, I have no idea how much we brought in but it must be huge. I am looking forward to that count. Then, after we fully wake up, we'll go out for brunch," he said hoping she would agree. She sipped her coffee and said, "After the clothes are done washing and I put them into the dryer, then we can go."

"I have a thought. Let's call Steve and tell him we will be there middle afternoon," said Robyn. "Since I will be working tomorrow, why don't we stop on our way to the Oasis and try to meet that bitch, or I mean that witch, Wendy...what's her fucking last name?"

"Stokey," answered Derrick. " Actually that sounds like a good plan. But let me do the talking."

"Why? Do you think I might shove that fucking curse down her fucking throat?" Robyn smuggley said.

"Yes! That is actually it! And she might turn you into a fucking frog or something." "Okay, okay. But if she pisses me off, I will tell her to go fuck herself."

"That'll work," he said sarcastically.

The drive to Desert Inn Estates in Las Vegas was not difficult, as the crowds were just coming alive after Saturday night's fling. Most people out and about were getting ready to leave, and new people were coming in as it is usual for Sundays.

As the Burns pulled into the Desert Inn Estates, they noticed how well maintained the homes and landscaping looked for not being a new community. Mainly the homes were modest in size, and mostly senior citizens lived here.

They did not even know if Wendy would be home but pressed the doorbell hoping she was. A lady, wearing a black, below the knee dress, maybe in her middle sixties, with mostly grey hair answered, "Who are you?"

"Hi, my name is Derrick, and this is my wife Robyn. We would briefly like to talk with you about, umm, a so-called, curse?" dragging the word as a question.

"Curse on what?" she asked.

"Could we please come in, just for a couple of minutes? It is getting a bit warm out here."

"Only for a couple of minutes. I am in the middle of making stew."

"Thank you," Derrick said.

Looking around the house Derrick noticed how dimly lit the small living room was. Many lit candles scattered around were mainly the light. Off into the kitchen was a black crystal type ball on the table with two large books. A black cat was sitting on the couch watching their every move. "Is your name Wendy?" he asked.

"Yes. Why are you here, and what questions do you have?"

"Robyn and I are the new owners of the Lucky Oasis Casino, and they tell us that there is some kind of curse that you might have put on the place."

"YES! YOUR DAMN RIGHT I PUT A CURSE ON IT!" shouted Wendy.

"Could you tell me why?" asked Derrick politely as he noticed Robyn frowning.

Wendy lifted her head saying, "My dear husband was killed there, THAT'S WHY!

Too bad you own that wicked place."

"Was that not an accident Wendy?"

"If they were more careful, he would not have tripped and fell. Just what this area needs, another casino."

"Wendy, we had nothing to do with what happened to your husband. We are just trying..."

"STOP! There is a curse on that awful place and that's that," she snapped.

"Are you maybe against casinos too?"

"I have had enough of your questions. Leave now."

Robyn couldn't hide it anymore saying, "Why don't you take one of your fucking lit candles and stick it up your ass!"

"Get out!" As Derrick and Robyn were heading to the door Wendy said, "Next Tuesday, the fourth of October, at (four o'clock in the afternoon) death bells will ring every minute until five along with amisty yellow smoke .

Enjoy your ownership."

The door was not completely closed when Robyn blurted out, "You are one disturbed mother fucker!"

Getting into the car Derrick said, "That went well."

As they drove to the Lucky Oasis Robyn nonchalantly said, "You know Derrick, I held off as long as I could. That fucked up, demented witch had no intention to even listen to you. She's very bitter and nuts. How long has it been since her husband died?"

He thought for awhile and said, "When the Oasis was built, that's well, that's four years before Tony bought it. Tony's death and Jack's death adding four years for each is, ahh, that's over twelve years ago."

"And the bitch still has not gotten over it," added Robyn.

"No she hasn't. Do you really think she is an actual witch? I mean, casting spells and such?"

Robyn firmly said, "She looks like a witch; she talks like a witch, her place looks like a witches den. Yeh, I'd say she is a fucking witch."

"Guess your right. But we had to try and talk with her. Let's just see how this plays out. Hey, we are together in one car, and you are going to work tomorrow.

Are you planning on staying at the Oasis until three?"

"Oh shit. You are right. We have one car, and I need to get home early. Doesn't

Steve leave early? Why can't I ask Steve to run me home?"

"We can ask. Just behave yourself." "Piss off, Derrick." He just smiled.

Derrick changing the subject said, "Hey Robyn, I got a thought about Country and Western nights at the Oasis. How about calling it 'Western Days'? We could have the employees including the dealers, and us too, wear western gear. Maybe we can offer some type of prize for the best western dressed gal. What do ya think?"

"Sounds interesting. Why don't we discuss this with Steve and see what he thinks?"

"Yeah, let's do that," he said.

Chapter

9

BUSINESS BOOMING

The Lucky Oasis Casino at three o'clock Sunday afternoon had several people in the Eatery and about fifteen players at the tables and slots. This was about normal for a Sunday as most of them were either leaving or going to Vegas. The out-of-towners enjoyed the Oasis by having something light to eat going each way from and to Vegas. Several liked to get their game warm-ups in on the low minimums.

Derrick and Robyn went up to the office to review Saturday's receipts. Steve was just setting up schedules for the week for the workers. Seeing the Burns walking into the office he said, "Nice to see you both. Must have been hectic last night."

"It was fucking jammed!" exclaimed Robyn.

Derrick added, "Yeh, I even helped out in the pit giving breaks."

"Steve, when you leave today, can you drop me off at my house?" asked Robyn.

"I, I guess."

"We did not get up until noon. We were tired and not thinking straight, I guess.

We took off in one car not realizing that I cannot stay here until 3:00 am."

"Sure Robyn. I have no problem taking you home."

Steve sat back in the desk chair saying, "Mostly on Friday and Saturday nights we have been getting pretty good crowds. What I heard about last night was that it was one of the biggest crowds we have ever had."

"It was fun and exhausting at the same time. No real complaints mind you. We will need to keep an eye on this and maybe we might have to add one or two part time employees. That brings to mind, what were the numbers last night?"

Steve stood up and said, "Let's go into the counting room and you can see for yourself."

The counting room door was in the office. Before they went in Derrick mentioned, "On our way here we stopped to see Wendy. The way her house looked she definitely thinks she is a fucking witch. She still is very bitter about her husband's death connected to the Oasis and would not entertain any discussion about the curse or anything. And with Robyn's delicate pitch of telling her to shove a lit candle up her ass, she gave us another curse."

Robyn added, "Yeh, yeh, she is one fucking demented bitch, or witch, or whatever you want to call her."

"What type of curse?" asked Steve. Derrick continued, "Some kind of death bells ringing next Tuesday, the fourth. Like the ones you mentioned before, Steve." Plus some type of yellowish smoke.

"Oh shit! Those bells! How long?"

"From four to five. Sixty minutes."

"Wholly shit! SIXTY MINUTES! Wait until you hear these god-for-shaken bells. And now, some type of yellow smoke. Good job, Derrick"

Steve unlocked the counting room door walking to the center table. "Here is the report." As they reviewed the report Derrick said, "This looks real good. Bottom line take was over twenty two thousand dollars!"

"That is almost a record," Steve adding, "We had just under twenty three thousand one night two months ago. That band, Silver Spurs, really draws in the people." Robyn taking all this in asked, "How much were expenses?"

"Not all the details concerning expenses have been accounted for right now, but I would say in the neighborhood of about five thousand would be a good guess. We should end up with about seventeen thousand profit for the night," said Steve.

Derrick asked, "Will the accountant be here tomorrow?"

"Yea, Jerry Duncan works from 8am to 5pm on Monday, Wednesday and Friday." "Great, I would like to meet him and go over some details. I'm planning on coming in at three or four in the afternoon. Please ask him not to leave until I get here." "No problem," answered Steve. "Also Steve, could we arrange that I come in late afternoons, say fourish and you open in the morning at seven and stay until I get here?"

"So you want me to work days?"

"Yes," said Derrick. "And I will close at 3 am. I would like to experience just what type of business we have during the night, for now, anyway.'"

"Steve, Derrick has an idea," said Robyn.

"Oh, what's that?"

"What do you think about calling Friday and Saturday nights, "Western Days?" We already have Country and Western bands now. We could all dress up in western attire. Maybe offer a prize for the best dressed cowgirl," suggested Derrick.

Steve reacted, "Sounds interesting. I am not sure how many more people we can bring into this place on weekend nights. You saw how packed we were last night."

"Yea, it was packed. But to stay packed, we need to come up with new ideas.

That really is the lifeblood of success," stated Derrick.

Robyn said, "And here I was the fucking event planner at the Starbrite and Derrick offers Western Days. I love it!"

Steve seemed to like the idea as well saying, "Okay, why don't we put together all the details and shoot for starting this in November? You know, after Halloween at the end of this month."

Robyn added, "Great, I will let the dealers and everyone else know what we are planning."

Robyn made up a letter (since she would only be working part time) informing all employees about the plans to have Western Days on Friday and Saturday nights. She said everyone needs to wear western type gear those two days. If anyone needed assistance purchasing such, just let Derrick or her know.

Steve mentioned that he wanted to leave by six. So he took Robyn home. On the way home Steve said to Robyn, "You ever think about sex with anyone else except Derrick? I mean, ohh, you know, just for something different?"

Robyn looking sharply at Steve answered, "No. I had my wild flings before I met Derrick. We love each other passionately and that is all we need."

"Please, I didn't mean anything or wasn't trying to hit on you. I was just courious you being such a beautiful, sexy looking girl, and all."

"Thanks for the compliment, Steve. Seems to me that you have a pretty good looking girl yourself with Sam."

"Yes. Sam and I are very good friends. Nothing very serious you know, just good friends."

"Thanks again, Steve for taking me home," said Robyn as she exited his car.

Derrick finished Sunday by closing the casino at 2:15am. He was tired and there were no players in the place. He arrived home just before 3am. He tried to be as quiet as possible so as not to wake Robyn.

Chapter

10

OCTOBER CURSES

It was almost noon on Tuesday, October fourth. After taking a shower and getting dressed, Derrick noticed a note from Robyn on the kitchen table. I will stop over at the Oasis after work. You can tell me if that damn curse went off. How about we get something to eat at The Eatery? That was good news for him. He then had some left over coffee with a danish he warmed up in the microwave. Checking his wallet he added one hundred dollars to it and headed out. Just then, before closing the door, the phone rang. It was Al saying all the documents were now completed and they could come by, at their convenience, to review and obtain copies.

Stopping on his way to the Lucky Oasis, he got an oil change and car wash. He arrived at the casino just after three. That was perfect as he wanted to be there to witness if this so called curse would really happen.

Steve was putting some finishing touches on a group of four progressive slots. Derrick saw him and went over to see how things were. Steve seeing him said, "You're here a little early."

"Yea, I wanted to go over some things with you and to see if that fucking curse of bells goes off at four. What's up with these slots?" "I am just double checking that all four of these progressive slots are hooked up properly. These are special penny wheel slots that pay a jackpot of $10,000 with max bet of three dollars. You cannot find any bigger jackpot payouts for just three dollar max bets anywhere. These are on loan from Bally as an experiment to see what type of action they deliver. This means no other casino has them, and we get fifty percent of the take."

"Nice. When you finish here, I'll be up in the office. ."

Steve found Derrick in the counting room. "How did your meeting go with Jerry yesterday?"

"It went well," Derrick said. "He seems like a nice, typical nerd, which is probably who we want working on the books. Umm, Steve, what do we have set up for Halloween? I know it is actually on Monday this year, but I am interested in what we have planned for Friday and Saturday that weekend."

"To tell you the truth, we really don't have anything planned, except we allow our employees to dress up somewhat if they want. We also have that spooky organ sound. But that is just on Halloween from four to midnight."

"Okay. I'll run this by Robyn and see if she thinks we should do something."

DONG. "There it is!" exclaimed Steve. "That loud, dull, bell sound. Right at four o'clock, on the button. Oh, there's that yellow smoke you mentioned."

Derrick said, "Let's go down to the casino to hear it." DONG. They both went down the stairs to the casino. DONG. "That is a loud, dull and annoying bell sound and the music has stopped. It is all quiet between the bell sounds."

DONG. "Yes! That is what happens when the bell tolls. Quiet. No sound," said Steve. Derrick shaking his head said, "Show me the sound system Steve." There is a door built into the side of the stairway. Inside is a small room that housed the furnace, air conditioning controls, electrical panel, lighting and sound system. As they were unlocking the door, DONG. "Damn, that is annoying," said Derrick.

Steve showed him the sound system. They tried turning down the volume, turning up the volume, and turning the system off. Nothing. DONG. "That's fucking unbelievable!" Derrick snapped sarcastically. "I can't believe that bitch is actually a witch. And that this DAMN curse is actually happening." DONG.

"FUCK!" Derrick appeared to be getting pissed. Yellow misty smoke was pouring out from the air vents.

"Did you say this will go on until five o'clock, Derrick?" "Yea. That's what that fucking witch said." DONG. Steve suggested, "We have some large floor fans in storage. Let's get them and place them facing the open door." After doing that, Derrick turned to Steve, "Do we have that music system piped into the office?" "No. But we have the sound system set up for us to make announcements. And guess what, that damn dull bell sound comes through there too." DONG. "Shit."

Derrick looked around the casino seeing maybe six or seven players. "The only good thing is we do not have many players. That damn bell and smoke will drive anyone to leave. DONG. How about in the lodge, Steve? Does this damn bell sound go on in there too?"

"No. That is the only place we can get away from it."

"Let's go to the lodge office, Steve, before I go fucking nuts." DONG.

Steve left for the day before Robyn arrived at 5:30. She was wearing a tight orange short skirt with four inch heels. As she strutted across the casino floor she looked absolutely stunning…especially after working eight hours. Seeing Derrick in the gaming pit she headed there. "Hi ya babe," said Derrick. "Hi." She gave him a kiss and then asked, "Can we get a drink?"

"Absolutely. You look really great!. Let's go to the lounge."

In the Oasis Lounge, Burt, just starting his bartender shift said, "What can I get for you gorgeous?"

Robyn smiled and said, "Frozen strawberry daiquiri." Derrick just took a Budweiser. He did not want anything strong as he would be working until three. They both went over to a booth. There were only two guys sitting at the bar so it was very quiet. Derrick went over to the Eatery and ordered two cheeseburgers. On his return to Robyn he said, "I got a call from Al. All the documents are in, and we can go review them anytime."

"Good, we will have to pick a day and go there. Tell me, Robyn asked, "What happened with the cursel thing?"

"It went off alright. It was very annoying and unsettling. Sixty loud dull bells rang, one for each fucking minute from four to five. Also we had a yellowish smoke fill the casino. Steve and I went to the lodge office to escape." "How many people experience this?" she asked.

"Thank God, only about six or seven," Derrick answered.

"Did you try and turn off the system or something?" asked Robyn taking a sip from her daiquiri.

"Yes. Steve and I went into the maintenance room under the stairs. We tried everything except shutting off all the power. That fucking bell kept ringing every minute. SIXTY LOUD TIMES, Robyn!"

"Oh my God! What do you think we can do about this?"

"I don't know, Robyn. I really don't know. Next up for this damn curse thing is Halloween. You know, the organ playing spooky tunes from four to midnight."

"That might not be such a big thing Derrick. Let me give that some thought. I just came over to see how that bell thing went off."

After finishing their cheeseburgers, Robyn said, "I had kind of a rough day and am a little tired. So if you don't mind, I want to get home and take a little swim. I'd like to review some options for that Halloween weekend, okay?"

"Yea, that's fine. I'll try and not wake you when I get home."

"That would be nice."

Robyn finished her drink. They hugged and kissed. He asked her to drive carefully.

October in Nevada delivered beautiful weather. Temperatures are usually in the eighties and low nineties. It was nearly noon on Saturday when Robyn, after breakfast, sat on the patio sipping coffee. The light breeze shuffled her blond hair gently as she tried to figure out what could be done for Halloween weekend. Still wearing her sheer pink pajama top and shorts, she decided to only decorate the Lucky Oasis with Halloweeen stuff. If the employees wanted to get moderately dressed up or not, that would be okay.

Derrick walked out to the patio yawning and stretching. "What's up?" he said half asleep.

"Just enjoying this nice weather sipping on coffee and thinking about Halloween.

Coffee is on. Want some breakfast?"

"Yea, if you don't mind making it."

"Not a problem. What do you want?"

"Got eggs and bacon?"

"Yep." Robyn got up went into the kitchen and started making his breakfast saying, "I decided that we will just decorate the Oasis for Halloween. Is that okay with you? How was last night?

He walked over and softly padded her firm behind and said, "Give me a kiss, babe." After kissing he said, "I support just about anything you want to do. As for last night, the crowd was good. Not jammed packed, but decent. We even had three rooms rented out.

Maybe after getting something to eat and waking up we can..."

"Have sex?" cutting him off.

"Yea. Before I go over to the Oasis."

"Then I won't get dressed." They both shared a smile.

Now fed, fully awake, and after some stimulating hot sex, Derrick getting dressed said, "You always make me feel so good, Robyn."

"Me too." Robyn always enjoyed having sex with him. Derrick really had a knack in satisfying her and she to him. It has never gotten old or just a chore.

Robyn said to Derrick, "I will go to the party store tomorrow and get some Halloween decorations. I will bring them over to the Oasis later."

"Perfect. Now let's go to the Oasis for, hopefully, a big Saturday night.

Saturday was busy. Not as wild as some Saturday nights, but a fun crowd no less. Robyn could now understand Derrick's thinking about doing new things. To keep the locals interested, the Lucky Oasis would need different theme's or promotions. This, of course, was right up Robyn's alley. Halloween would be her first challenge.

After getting home around 4am from the Saturday night fling, both Derrick and Robyn rolled out of bed at noon. Derrick wanted to take it easy before heading back to the Oasis. So, instead of going out for brunch, he along with Robyn, had a huge breakfast. He then went out to the patio to read the newspaper. Robyn was busy making up a list of Halloween items to buy.

At 3:30pm Derrick left for the Oasis. Robyn had already went Halloween shopping. Late afternoon on Sundays at the Lucky Oasis were very quiet. Those going and coming from California were now at their destinations. Locals stayed home for the most part. There were two people playing blackjack with maybe four playing slots. The lounge had three guys at the bar watching baseball playoffs. No one was in the Eatery. Derrick thought he might close up early if no one was around later.

Robyn walked in with a bunch of Halloween decorations. She asked Derrick to help her with getting pumpkins from her car. "Looks like you had some fun." "Yes I did. I plan on putting some decorations up now for a few hours. The rest during the weeknights. Where are the people?"

"Sundays, late afternoon are super slow according to Steve," Derrick said, If we have no one later, I might just close up for the night. You know what tomorrow is?" he asked.

"No, what?"

"Monday night we will have a full moon. That's when our damn lights are suppose to go off and on flashing for God knows how long."

"Oh shit. We just got over the fucking bells, now this."

"We will see how many people we have here on Monday at midnight. If it is like tonight, maybe I'll close up again.

"You know Derrick, as for Halloween, I will put "Spooky music for Halloweeen" on our marquee. Maybe that will help."

"Good idea," he said.

Next day, Derrick walked into the Oasis at 3:30 on Monday to talk with Steve. He met him working on a ceiling light in the Eatery. "What's with that light?"

Steve looking down from the ladder said, "Just tightening up the socket and putting in a new bulb. You know that there is a full moon tonight."

"Yes I know, Steve. I plan on closing early if we have no one here."

He took down the ladder, put it in storage and said, "We really should not close before 3 am, Derrick. But that is up to you. Do you need me for anything right now?" "I don't think so Steve. I will let you know how the light flickering worked out."

Right at midnight all the lights flickered on, off, on, off and stopped at 12:20am. It was a little nerve-racking but did not seem to cause any problems. Burt was resetting the tv's. The baseball games were over, and no one was in the lounge. In fact, there was no one anywhere.

Derrick told Burt to close down the lounge and went over to the cashier, closing and locking it up. He then signaled the two dealers to close the blackjack and roulette tables. The two dealers said thanks and timed out. The Eatery closed just before midnight.

The security officer with Derrick locked the chip covers, removed the cash boxes and toke boxes taking them to the counting room. Everyone was now gone, so Derrick said good night to the officer and double-checked all doors before leaving.

Robyn arranged an early out on Halloween from the Starbrite, so she could get to the Lucky Oasis by 3:30. Derrick arrived just before she did and was up in the counting room with Jerry, the accountant. Since it was the end of the month, financial reports would be due. Jerry suggested to Derrick to let him come in Tuesday so he could finalize all the reports. He agreed and seeing Robyn downstairs in the gaming pit, he went to her.

Robyn wore blue silk slacks with a short sleeve silk blouse and was talking with Steve who was watching the pit action. There were seven players playing various table games making moderate to high bets. Derrick entered the pit saying to Robyn, "I did not know you would be here so early."

"Yeah, wanted to hear that spooky organ music. Also, I want to leave soon to get some groceries. We have some nice action here with Steve supervising," she said.

"It's a good thing, said Derrick. I also noticed several slot players and three persons in the Eatery as well. "Want something to eat or drink?"

Nodding her head she said, "Yeah, let's get a drink before that damn organ starts playing."

As soon as it was 4:00, the music stopped and weird organ sounds started up. It was everywhere. That creepy slow groaning loud organ sound. It was not the kind you hear in church but the kind you hear in dense horror flicks. Even though it was Halloween, the sounds were not very pleasant. Derrick took Robyn over to the small maintenance room and tried again to shut off the sound system, to no avail. "I can't stop it Robyn," he said.

Robyn putting two fingers one in each ear said, "That is fucking shitty organ sounds. Are you going to be able to hear that until midnight?"

"If we don't have any table game players, I just might go into the lodge office." "Shit. I don't think I could listen to that fucking sound for eight hours," she said.

As they left the maintenance room they looked around and saw several people had already left. "Look at that, Derrick. We are losing players!"

Two more slot players were walking out the door as Derrick said, "Yeah, and we cannot do anything about it. This is our October fucking curse month for sure!"

Robyn added, "Remember I said three years from this Halloween if we cannot get these damn curses eliminated, it's good bye Lucky Oasis."

"I hope we can last that long."

Chapter 11

WESTERN DAYS

After October's curses, November is a welcomed sight. With the full moon expected on the eighth of the month, which is a Tuesday, flickering lights for twenty minutes, should be easier to take. Now they were eagerly ready to see how "Western Days" would pan out.

Robyn worked until noon on this Friday so she could get home and change into her western garb. She suggested packing a brief overnight bag in case they were too tired to drive home at 3:30 or 4am. This would make sense as they would be at the Oasis on Saturday late as well. They both planned a brief visit to Sophia on their way to the Lucky Oasis.

Sophia was glad to see them. She said her girlfriends took her shopping. She now had plenty of groceries and meds and felt good, and said not to worry about her. Sophia noticed they were dressed in western clothes and said," Is that how they dress at the casino these days?" Robyn said that they were putting on a "Western Days" theme so most people would be wearing cowboy boots and hats and such.

They were glad to hear that she was doing well. Derrick mentioned that a deposit was made into her checking account from the Oasis funds. She appreciated what they were doing and said Jack would be very pleased. They let her know that they would be checking in with her from time to time.

This was the first of four weekends for "Western Days." All employees including Derrick and Robyn were dressed in western gear. Robyn wore a mini blue jean skirt with a beige solid lace V-Neck long sleeve blouse showing a lot of cleavage. She also wore a brown cowboy hat and boots. Derrick put on jeans and a blue western shirt with his black cowboy boots and hat.

Steve saw them as they walked into the casino. "Whooa, what a sexy good looking cowgirl you are!" he said to Robyn.

"Thanks Steve. Looking forward to this," Robyn said.

Steve said he wanted to stay for awhile to see how "Western Days" would do. Right at 4pm the music stopped. DONG. "What the fuck," said Robyn. "Why is that damn bell sounding now?" she asked. DONG.

"I know this is the fourth of November, but we never had that in November before," said Steve.

Derrick thought, "I can't believe that maybe the fucking witch made that damn bell go off on EVERY fourth of the month!" DONG. "Looks like that may be the case."

Robyn exclaimed, "This is Friday and the first day of 'Western Days.' We don't need any fucking curse bullshit screwing that up!" DONG.

"Hopefully it will stop at five," added Steve.

Derrick looking frustrated said, "We are going to have to do something about this." DONG.

The bells stopped at five, and the regular music started back up. Steve looking at Derrick and Robyn said, "Glad those damn bells stopped. Let's not have that ruin our 'Western Days' weekend."

Derrick with a sigh of relief added, "You are right, Steve. Let's put that damn bell and fucking curse shit behind us, and have a good night." Robyn, still a little pissed, agreed.

The six o'clock crew was now arriving. All of them wore some type of western gear and most had cowboy hats on. Sam looked stunning in her skin tight jeans, V-Neck white blouse showing cleavage, but not as much as Robyn's. Her heavy make-up, long black hair under a black cowgirl hat made her a standout beauty. In fact, all six female dealers looked good. This was always a thing with Steve and Jack; that the weekend night dealers had to be good looking. It helped bring in the players.

All three, Derrick, Robyn and Steve walked over to the games the dealers were at and thanked them for wearing western gear. Robyn said, "We hope this works out well. We want everyone to have fun and make some money."

One blackjack girl, Crystal, asked Robyn "Are you going to have any contests, like best dressed cowgirl?"

"Good question, Crystal. Derrick said something about that some time back. Being so busy, we just didn't follow up on it. Do you think that would be a good idea?"

"I think so. You know, guys like looking at and voting on girls in costumes and such," said Crystal.

"Best dressed cowgirl or best sexy dressed cowgirl?" inquired Robyn.

Crystal thought for a second then said, "Ahh, probably best dressed sexy cowgirl providing it's not too raunchy. The way you are dressed, if I were a guy, I would definitely vote for you."

"Thank you, Crystal. Do you think I'm dressed too raunchy?

"Naw. You look good, sexy yes, but not raunchy."

"I value your input, Crystal. I'll let you know what we can work up."

As Crystal started opening her blackjack table, she wondered if she over stepped her comments.

The Friday night crowd was good. It was not swelling or over crowded but good. Mostly local young to middle aged guys and gals attended, which was about usual. At about ten thirty, Robyn got on stage. She introduced herself to many whistles and cheers. She asked if they should conduct a best sexy dressed cowgirl contest next week? A lot of yelling, whistling and clapping erupted. One guy yelled out, "Like you?" "I guess that's a yes," smiling she said over the microphone. "Okay, ya'all. We will put together some cash for winners. Have fun the rest of the night and see ya'all next week." She waved, exiting the stage to more whistles and yelling. Robyn walked back to the pit where Crystal was dealing. She waited until Crystal finished her hand saying, "Did you hear that?"

Crystal said, "I heard a lot of whistling and yelling."

"I asked the crowd if they would like a best sexy dressed cowgirl contest next week. That is why you heard all that noise. Two guys at Crystal's table looking at and overhearing Robyn said, "If the girls are dressed like you, count us in." They both smiled and Robyn said to Crystal, "In your pay next week you will find a $100 bonus for your idea."

"Wooa. Thank you Robyn!"

Steve went up to Robyn saying, "Hey sexy cowgirl, now you want a sexy cowgirl contest? I think that might be very interesting. I can't wait to see that. I've got to leave now so I can open at 7am tomorrow."

"Have a nice, safe night, Steve."

Maybe thirty to forty percent of those attending wore western gear of some sort. Everyone appeared to have a good time. Robyn felt that bringing in a best sexy dressed cowgirl contest would boost not only the attendance but offer something different.

At closing, Derrick and Robyn were tired. They both pitched in working and were glad they made arrangements to stay there overnight. When they finished putting the cash boxes away and seeing that everything was locked up, Derrick said, "Hey babe, are you too tired for a little western romp?" Robyn snapped back, "Never too tired to take on your big hot rod." Walking over to the lodge room Derrick said to Robyn, "How and why did you come up with this best dressed cowgirl contest?" "Best *'sexy'* dressed cowgirl contest," correcting him. "In talking with the dealers, Crystal asked if we planned on something like that. I said you had that idea some time ago, and we just never followed up on it. I thought it was a good idea and floated the question out to the crowd. Their reaction was swift and loud. Did you not hear that?

"Yea I did."

So, yes, I decided that we try it next week."

"Just like that. Not even asking me what I thought of the idea."

"Well, fuck, what would you have said, NO?"

"Just thought we are partners. Coming up with ideas and discussing them together before acting them out on our own. Remember, we are under the direction of Watson & Peters. I am sure something like a contest would be perfectly fine. But we do have to run changes past Al for guidance."

"You are right. You are always fucking right. So fire me."

"Robyn, don't act so damn stupid. I'm just saying…"

"I know, I know, we have to run this shit by Al."

"Yes. We need to see him anyway. Those final documents and title need our review. We can bring up your contest idea then. I will call him Monday to set up an appointment."

"Okay. Right now let's get into that fucking room so I can ride your big hot rod."

It was just after noon when they both woke up. Freshing up somewhat, they got dressed and went to the Omelet House for a late breakfast. They were pleased how the first Western Day went off. Robyn was jotting down ideas for future weekends as Derrick was driving to the restaurant.

Chapter
12

SECOND WITCH VISIT

Now they were still in their western clothes when Derrick said to Robyn, "Dressed a little sexy for the Omelet House, don't you think?"

"Oh shit, Derrick. I have a different outfit for tonight and I will change when we get back to the Oasis. Here, I'll fold my arms on my chest. Does that work for you?"

During breakfast Robyn said, "These damn curses are getting to me. Those bells that came on yesterday at 4pm on November fourth had never happened before. That might mean that nasty bitch of a witch can change her curses when the hell she wants to."

"So, what are you saying?" he inquired.

"What I am saying Derrick is it seems she can make up or do what the hell she wants, as to making up bullshit curses. What if she decides that it will not be four years between deaths in April. What if she makes it *this April*?"

"So, you are saying she may change the so-called four year death curse in April, to this April. Which would only be one year from when Jack died."

"Exactly," she said.

"Wholly shit. That is something we need to contemplate," said Derrick.

One more thing Robyn. I think I had a dream last night. Jack was saying thanks for taking over the Lucky Oasis and helping his mother. He also said hang in there. Things will be alright."

She stared into Derrick's eyes saying, "Wonder what that means."

Leaving the restaurant while walking to the Forester, Derrick said, "Do you think we should try just one more time to make a visit to Wendy the witch?"

"What the hell do you think that would achieve?" asked Robyn.

Derrick thought for a minute before answering, "We could quickly run by the house so you could find something else to wear. Then we could pick up a nice bottle of Merlot wine as a gift and make an appeal to her.

"Bullshit. We can pick up the wine but if she does not like my mini skirt or blouse, fuck her."

"Robyn, we really need to try and ask her, in a nice way, to remove that fucking curse."

"You saw what the bitch did last time we tried this," she said.

"Yeah, I know, I know. "But we need to try again. I like running the Lucky Oasis and don't want to give that up. Don't you want to continue with the Oasis?"

"Yes, I do. I guess you are right. It won't hurt to give that bitch one last chance."

"If she is home," Derrick said and went on, "maybe I should just make the call and you stay in the car. That way you don't have to worry about how you're dressed."

"I'm not fucking worried about that. I will stay in the car, just for you. Keep it simple and don't come back with another damn curse."

Derrick pulled up to Wendy's house. Took the wine and rang her door bell. Wendy was home and answered, "Whooo, oh, you again."

"Hi Wendy. I'm Derrick and would like to talk with you briefly. Here is a bottle of Merlot wine."

She took the wine and said, "How did you know that Merlot was one of my favorite wines?"

"Lucky guess," he said.

"Alright, you can come in for just a spell."

Derrick said, "Thank you. For just a 'spell'?"

"Figure of speech," Wendy said with a small smile.

Derrick sensing she appeared to be in good 'spirits' as she picked up her cat and sat down, he went right to what he wanted to say. "Wendy, I believe you are a good person and do not want to harm innocent people. Right?" "Of course," she answered.

"Well, when my good friend Jack died, as the owner of the Lucky Oasis, he bequeathed to my wife and I the Oasis. We are managing that casino not only for our benefit, but also Jack's mother. We need to see that she receives a good portion of the profits every year. I am asking if you would reconsider the curses you have on the Lucky Oasis."

"You said you are managing the Lucky Oasis and not the owners?" she asked. Derrick said, "It is somewhat complicated; in that, yes, we are managing it but we are also considered 'conditional owners'."

"What do you mean conditional owners?"

"My wife and I must see that one half of the profits are taken out for Jack's mother and the casino's emergency fund. We will only be getting fifty percent of the profits. If we do not fulfill these requirements, we lose any ownership."

"Sounds like you may have made a bad decision. The curses on that place have to do with them being negligent and causing my husband to lose his life. That has caused me deep sorrow and loneliness. I made a promise to my dear husband to avenge his death. Besides, when a curse is made, it cannot be unmade. Only another curse on top of it can change it. If I were you, I would get out of that decision to take over the Lucky Oasis. If you do, no curse will fall onto you."

"Wendy, it has been over twelve years now since that accident. We are very sorry about what happened to your husband. We did not have any control or anything to do with that accident. We never dreamed we would be in the position to run a casino. We were asked to help out Jack's mother by running his casino. Three people have died, plus your husband, during the last twelve years. Is this what you want, more deaths? Hasn't there been enough of that already?"

Staring into Derrick's eyes while petting her black cat she said, "You should just forget about this casino and get out of it before it is too late. No curse will befall you if you do. I'm sorry you got yourself into this. Our discussion on this is now finished."

Derrick shaking his head said, "I'm sorry you feel that way Wendy. Looks like you prefer evil over good. I will do anything and everything to help my good friend Jack and his mother by keeping that casino promise."

"Good bye Derrick, and thank you for the wine." Wendy said.

As Derrick was getting into the car, Robyn asked, "Well, how did the visit go with that fucking witch?"

"Not too productive. At least she was receptive. She said for us to get out of ownership before it is too late."

"Too late? Meaning her death curse?" Robyn quickly asked.

"Something like that. I will make an appointment with Al on Monday. We need to inform him of what has taken place."

"Are we going to give this up like the piece of shit witch said?"

"That may be a possiblity. Let's just wait and see what Al thinks. Right now we are going to the Lucky Oasis for Saturday's Western Day festivities. We need to be positive and forget this for now."

"You know Derrick, why can't we just do something or have a little fun without bullshit complications? It's fucking aggravating. But, I agree, let's put this out of our minds for tonight." Robyn said.

The first order of business when arriving at the Lucky Oasis was to contact Steve for any information. There were no problems or no employee call offs; thank God. They told Steve about the second meeting with Wendy the witch. Derrick purposely kept the part of

Wendy telling them to give up the casino from the discussion. They now devoted their time preparing for the Saturday night crowd.

The second day of Western Days was a little disappointing. It was not jammed or over crowded. Maybe fifty or sixty less people attended than usual. For the most part, everyone seemed to have fun. Again, Robyn mentioned having a sexy western dressed cowgirl contest next weekend to many cheers.

Chapter 13

LEGAL CONSULTATION

Late Monday morning Derrick got a hold of Al at Watson and Peters Law Firm. He was able to set an appointment for 1:30 on Friday. He immediately called Robyn to see if she could get Friday off. Later that day, she called him to say there was no problem getting off. This would work out well, as they could just head over to the Lucky Oasis after the meeting.

Tuesday was a full moon night. Right at midnight all the lights flickered off and on for twenty minutes. Derrick noticed some slot machines operating erratically to the lights flashing on and off.
Many machines were on steady due to their battery backups. When the flickering was over, everything seemed normal. This curse was more of a nuisance than a hindrance.

Being midnight on a weekday, Derrick noticed two or three slot players, one person at 3-card poker, and two at blackjack were not fazed about the lights flickering. At 1:10 the last two players left. Derrick closed the casino and drove home.

Robyn got up first this Friday. She went right into the kitchen so as not to wake Derrick. She made coffee and toast for breakfast and went outside on the patio to read the newspaper and finish her breakfast. Derrick walked out to the patio around ten with coffee in hand. "Good morning sunshine," he said to Robyn. "I could not sleep any longer. I plan on catching up with the mail and pay some bills. What do you plan on doing?"

"The wash. A little cleaning up here and there. What time do we need to meet with Al?"

"Our meeting is at 1:30. You know we need to put on our western gear before leaving," he said.

"Yea, I know. Derrick, what the fuck are we going to say to Al about this whole curse thing?"

Derrick said, "I gave this a lot of thought last night, Robyn. As we were not very busy, I glanced around the casino just thinking how great this is to actually run and possibly own this real casino. It would be so exciting making a go of the place. Especially with our gaming experience. But then, facing and putting up with these damn curses, one that could even lead to our death. I thought maybe we should really think about what we are doing. Is it worth it?"

Robyn said, "Should we contact the police on these curse threats?"

"Robyn," Derrick shaking his head said, "Do you honestly believe the cops would entertain investigating a witch? They probably would think we are nuts. Funny thing, up to this time I never believed in witchcraft or curses. Hell, this is the real world. That was just fantasy, make believe. Now here we are facing a real witch. Facing a real curse. Honestly, I can't fucking believe it."

"I can't either. I hear what you are saying. Shit, we have only managed the casino for a couple of months. We are now just going to the lawyer's office to sign the ownership papers. DAMN! And now we are thinking about giving that all up." "Robyn, you are right. This is just November. Maybe we should keep going for two or three more months. Let's see how we can manage it all. Come next February, if we are still frustrated with the curses, then hang it up." Robyn shaking her head affirmately, "That sounds like a plan. We need to share all this with Al and see what he thinks."

Derrick and Robyn were again greeted by the receptionist saying, "Al is ready for you; go right in. Al standing up said, "Nice to see you both. Cowboy hats and boots; you look real western."

"Yep," said Derrick "That is the theme we have for the Lucky Oasis on Friday and Saturdays. We call it Western Days, hoping everyone will come dressed in western gear. We also are having a best dressed sexy cowgirl contest."

Al looking at Robyn said, "Looks like you should win that." Noticing her white, tie front, lace trim, crop top revealing her belly button. With her tight jeans, she really looked the part of a sexy cowgirl.

"No, no Al, I can't win it. This contest is for guests only."

"Is there a prize for the winner?" asked Al.

"Yes. The first place winner gets $100, second place $50 and third place $25. We are just trying to stimulate attendance with new ideas," she said.

"That sounds like it will be titillating fun. Take some pictures. As for the contest money, that amount should not be a problem. You know that you are working on only fifty percent of the profits. So just be a little careful," mentioned Al.

Al pulled out a file saying, "Are you ready to review your title and license as ownership of the Lucky Oasis?"

Derrick glancing at Robyn said, "I think we are Al. However, we want to share with you some experiences that have taken place. Actually, they have made us a little edgy."

"What kind of experiences?" Al asked.

Derrick continued, "That curse we talked about, well, we've come to believe it is real. In fact, there are several curses. First is the monthly curse. On full moon nights, at midnight, all the lights flicker on and off for twenty minutes. It does not seem to cause any damage. It's just a nuisance. Then there is the funky organ sounds that play from 4pm until midnight on Halloween. It comes through our sound system and cuts off the music. So far, that is the only time it has come on. But the organ sounds are beyond spooky. They are downright aggravating. If that sound happens only on Halloween, we probably could live with it. Next is the loud, dull, death bell sound. Once again, the music is cut off. It is silent except for that bell sound, every minute for sixty minutes. Steve said before it only happened on April 4th for twenty minutes. Now, since we visited Wendy, the witch, the bell sound and a new yellow smoke lasted for a full hour. You can't believe how upsetting that is. Even players have left when that happens."

Al looked a little puzzled asking, "You visited a witch? A real witch?"

Robyn wanted to say something but Derrick would not let her answering, "That's right. A *real* witch. A spooky house, with lit candles everywhere for light, and a black cat."

Robyn finally added, "A pissed off witch that will not back down. She will not even listen to reason. She just says get out of that place, as she strokes her damn black cat."

"I see that this Wendy has gotten under your skin also," said Al.

"Let me put it this way. That wacked bitch of a witch can add or change her curses, it seems, whenever she fucking wants to. My biggest concern is that she may change the *death curse* that happens on April 4 every four years, to NEXT APRIL. And if we are the owners of the Lucky Oasis, Derrick, me, or both, could die of some cause from it."

Al, sitting with his mouth open as he listened to all this said, "This looks like it has added a new twist to this whole thing. It seems to me that these curses and that witch have you both really spooked."

"Al," Derrick breaking in, "Robyn and I really like Jack's casino and want to try and make a go of it. Yes, we are spooked by these curses. However, we would like to continue on for the next two or so months. Just to see if we can manage the casino while putting up with these curses. Maybe trying to get them somehow changed or eliminated." Al sitting back in his chair, listened intently at what Derrick was saying.

"Since the license and title are now complete, let's say, two or three months from now, we find out that we just cannot continue. Can't we just sell or turn the Lucky Oasis back to Watson and Peters?" asked Derrick.

Al reviewed the current documents and looked over the Lucky Oasis file. After several minutes he said, "Yes, yes you can sell the casino. In light of your ownership being conditional, the title contains a lien to our firm, until all conditions have been settled. This means that if you want to sell the Lucky Oasis, your title would be assigned back to Watson and Peters. We then, would have the responsibilities to liquidate the property. The Lucky Oasis has no mortgage so when it is sold, there would be no lien notes.

Jack also made additional requirements in his offer to you. In the event, you could not, or did not, want to accept or continue with the conditional ownership, that ownership would revert back to Watson and Peters. All proceeds collected from the sale of the Lucky Oasis would go to his mother, if still alive. Two hundred and fifty thousand dollars would be taken out of the sale and given to you both. In the event Jack's mother was not alive, all proceeds, except your two hundred and fifty thousand, would go to selected charities that he has designated. So you can see, Jack still wanted to thank you for just considering helping his mom and keeping the Lucky Oasis going. He knew there may be some challenges that might come up to prevent you from fulfilling the requirements in his conditional ownership."

"That is certainly generous of Jack offering us that kind of money if we walk away from it all. For sure, that lifts a lot of pressure off our minds, " said Robyn.

"I totally agree," added Derrick. "Still, we want to try and make a go of this. It would be nice to fulfill all the conditions and own the casino outright. However, it is reassuring knowing that if we cannot, we still would get two hundred fifty thousand bucks for trying. What a great friend Jack was!"

Al added, "I held back in telling you about this little perk, until I was convinced that you both would try and make Jack's wish come true."

"It still might, Al. Robyn and I will give it our best shot. We will only come back to see you on this if we cannot do everything within our means to make it work out. I may even try offering that damn witch a bribe."

"I am sure you both will do your best. Just be careful on using bribes. Do it only with cash, so there is no paper trail. Do you have anymore questions?" asked Al.

"Just one more Al. I know we need to contact you on any changes we would like to make. Since it has been extremely slow on most weekday nights, I have decided to close the casino early, like at one or one-thiry. Is that okay?" asked Derrick.

"It has been known for a long time, that the Lucky Oasis is open every day until three am. So if you close at one and a group of four guys come at 1: 30 to do some gaming and you are closed, that is not good. As you know, in the Vegas area casinos are usually open 24 hours every day. I am not suggesting that you stay open for 24 hours, but for now I would keep the casino open until 3am. Maybe you could close the kitchen or bar early on any given day. But I would keep the casino open as it has been for years."

"I have one question Al," said Robyn. What if we have to turn the casino back to you, and you sell it. Do you have to tell the new buyer about the damn curses?"

"Good question, Robyn. I will have to give that a lot of thought."

"Just saying." Robyn smiling then added, "Thanks Al for all your input and help." "Yes, thanks Al. We will be in touch," finished Derrick.

"Have fun at your Western Days." Al waved goodbye.

Chapter 14

COWGIRL CONTEST

After more then two hours at the law office, the Burns walked into the Lucky Oasis just after four. Derrick went directly to the office without even noticing there were about ten players at various games. Robyn went over to the lodge counter to see if there were any rooms reserved. She then went into their sleeping room to relax for a while. Seeing Steve at the office desk Derrick asked, "Everything in order? All banks and schedules set up?"

"Nice to see you too," said Steve. "Yes, everything is ready to go. There are no call offs. We have a full staff tonight."

"Great. Sorry we are a little late. We spent more time at the lawyer's office than we thought. It is now official. We have the title and license finalized.

Would you like to join Robyn and I for something to eat before you take off?"

"Thanks. I really planned on staying to see the 'sexy cowgirl contest' if it starts early enough. So, yes, I will join you guys. You are staying on then, as owners, curse or no curse?"

"Right now, Steve. We will see how this all plays out."

As they went down the stairs to the Eatery, Derrick looked around for Robyn. He saw her coming from the lodge entrance and said, "Steve will join us for dinner and he plans on staying for the contest."

"Super. Hi Steve," she said.

"Man, you really know how to dress for tonight! Hope the contest is not too late," Steve said.

Robyn gave him a sexy smile saying, "I plan on conducting the contest right after the bands first set. Do you think I'm dressed too sexy?"

"Not for me. You always look terrific," said Steve.

"Okay, are you guys now done yaking? Can we go and get something to eat?" asked Derrick.

As they were eating Derrick asked Robyn, "What were you doing over by the lodge?"

Robyn answered, "I needed a little rest. Also, we need to register the contestants. So I made a sign that says, 'Register Here For Best Sexy Dressed Cowgirl Contest'. I also put a small sign at the main entrance. I plan on staying at that counter until 9:30 to register the girls."

Steve said, "Can I help you there?"

"Nice try, Steve. But, wait, that may be a damn good idea. After we get done eating, you can help me put together what we need to do," she said.

"And I was going to ask for a raise," a smiling Steve said.

"If you both can find some time, I am available to help out too," said Derrick. Robyn seeing his pathetic looking face said, "I really don't need that much help in the registering. When it comes time to bringing the girls on the stage, I could use your help at that time, sweety. Up until then, I think you will be plenty busy." Derrick was at the gaming pit complimenting on how good everyone looked. They all wore western wear. Once again, Sam stood out with her tastefully sexy attire. The tables were about half full nearing seven thirty. That indicated they should have a big crowd.

Robyn registered one girl, Sally, that wore tight black jeans, pink print V-neck short top and, of course, black boots and hat. Steve would make up a small sticky nametag for the girls first name. The girls would hold their name above their head when the voting would start. All girls entering the contest must register before nine thirty.

This weekend the band, Wild Horse, would perform. It is a very popular country rock band, just like Silver Spurs. Nearing nine o'clock the place was pretty packed. Robyn was finishing up registering the contestants. She now had five girls registered. Steve was in his glory viewing the girls and making up their nametags. All the girls, naturally, were gorgeous. Sam walked by, going on her break, giving Steve that female eye. She said to him, "Better watch yourself, sugar." He just smiled.

The band started a little late, at nine fifteen, so their first set ended just passed ten. Robyn entered the stage taking the mic saying, "Good evening ya'all. Ready for the Oasis Lounge first 'Best Sexy Dressed Cowgirl Contest?" The yelling and whistling was deafening. The entire lounge was jammed packed with many people standing outside. "Get ready, now, to meet six gorgeous cowgirls."

Steve and Derrick directed the six girls, one by one, onto the stage standing side by side. The cheers got even louder. Robyn shaking her head said, "Ya'all, here is how the contest will work. Each girl will step forward with her name above her head. You then vote with cheers, clapping and whistling. We will do this for all six of these beautiful cow girls. Derrick, (taking a bow) Steve (the same) and I will judge which gal gets the loudest vote. The first place girl is awarded $100, second place $50 and third $25."

The place was absolutely in a frenzy. It was very difficult chosing the winners, as the cheers and noise was nearly as loud for each beautiful girl. Finally, a top winner was chosen. A long brown-haired girl wearing a white bikini top, very short jean shorts with knee high boots and cowgirl hat won the $100. After awarding the $50 to the second place girl, Robyn said, "All these beautiful gals deserve an award. So, we are awarding $25 to each of the four remaining gals."

Never, ever, has the Oasis Lounge been so crazy loud as it was this night.

After the contest was over, Robyn went to their overnight room in the lodge. That room also served as the break room for all employees. She layed down on the bed as she was experiencing a slight headache. Steve walked into the room and said, "Good job, Robyn, with that contest. You feeling alright?"

"Yes, Steve. Just a little tired with a slight headache."

"Hope you feel better soon. I will be leaving for the night. However, if you would like me to help you feel better …"

"Good night, Steve."

"Just saying." As he left. The bell for rooms sounded. Robyn got up and went to the lodge counter. A couple standing there said they would like to reserve a room for the night. This now made six rooms booked for the night. After registering them, she then went to the lounge to see if help was needed.

It was just before midnight when Derrick went to the lodge office room. He got a coffee and just needed a break from all the noise and partying going on. Sam walked by, seeing the office door somewhat opened, looked in. Seeing Derrick at the desk with his head in his arms she said, "Everything okay, Derrick?"

Looking up he said, "Yes, Sam. Just trying to unwind and get a break from all the noise."

"Do you need me to rub your neck or something?"
"No, I am fine. Thank you anyway," he said.

"Well, call me if you need me. I'll just be in the next room on my break."

Robyn seeing Sam going to the lodge for her break, thought that she would join her. She noticed Sam leaving the office room heading to the break room. She went into the office seeing Derrick leaning way back in the desk chair and said,

"What's that all about?"

"Whats what all about?" he said.

"Sam just left here."

"Yea. She asked me if I was alright. Don't you go thinking now some shit is going on here."

"Me? Naw, I was just curious, Derrick. How *are* you feeling?'

"I am fine, Robyn. Just came here to get a break from all the noise. And you did a great job with that contest."

"Thank you. Maybe we should add the Best Dressed Cowboy Hunk Contest?"

"Oh please, Robyn. Wait until tomorrow for this. Okay?"

"Fine. I was just going to our other room for a break with Sam. Unless you want me to stay with you?"

"Nice thought. But I'm just ready to go back out there. I know one thing, we're staying here tonight. This crowd is one, big, fun loving, partying group. We still got about two fucking hours to go, and I am already tired."

"Okay. See you later. I'll check out the gaming tables and see if we can close some of them down."

Derrick gave her a reassuring kiss as he left.

The Wild Horse band stopped playing at 2:30. The PA announced at 2:45, "Thank you for partying with us. The casino will close in fifteen minutes. Please Drive Carefully." This Friday night everyone came out to party and have fun, and it was going to be a chore getting all of them out. One by one, with the help of the security officer, they were able to close down.

Derrick, Robyn and Tom, the gaming pit supervisor, closed out the remaining table games. They locked all the doors and let Tom and the security officer out. Derrick said, "Wow, what a night!"

"You are not fucking kidding. Plus it was *curse free*. Let's get to our room," said Robyn. They had to be sure the lodge door into the casino was locked as six rooms were occupied that night.

Robyn just finished washing up as Derrick went in to do the same. Robyn got under the covers completely naked. When Derrick turned off the lights and pulled down the covers to get in bed, Robyn kissed him saying, "How about a quicky?"

"Are you not beat?" he said. "A little, but don't worry, I'll get on top."

During their sleep just before waking up, the room got very cold. Robyn, still not wearing anything, reached for more covers when she saw what appeared to be a transparent figure. It looked like the witch, Wendy, hovering above the bed. "Abandon this cursed casino," she heard it say in a echo, hollowed sound. Robyn rubbed her eyes, but the moving see-through figure was still there saying again, "Abandon this cursed casino, or you shall die." Frightened, she shook

Derrick saying," Wake up, wake up Derrick." As soon as he woke, the transparent figure disappeared.

Derrick not fully awake, said, "Ohh, what's up."

"Did you see that?" she said.

"See what Robyn?" he asked.

"That semi see-through Wendy the witch. She was just there, above our bed," said a trembling Robyn.

"No. I don't see anything, Robyn. Why is it so cold in here?" he asked.

Robyn, still shaking blurted out, "She was there. She, she said get out of this cursed casino."

Derrick seeing that Robyn was all shook up and trembling, put his arm around her while pulling up some covers and said, "Maybe you had a bad dream. Here, get under the covers and try to go back to sleep." Due to good drapes, the room was very dark. He looked at the clock showing 8:15am saying, "There is no one here. You must of had a dream. Let's try and get back to sleep." "It was no dream," Robyn said as she snuggled next to Derrick and closed her eyes.

Chapter
15

HELP NEEDED

Robyn, fully dressed, was sitting on the desk chair when Derrick woke up. Seeing her he asked, "How long have you been up?"

"Since ten," she said.

Looking at the clock seeing it was 11:30 he said, "Why didn't you wake me?"

"I just wanted you to get as much sleep as you could."

"Well thanks, but..."

Robyn looking stern broke in, "That was no dream Derrick. That was no dream what I saw and heard."

Trying to figure out how he could sooth her he said, "Remember when I said I had a dream about Jack saying don't worry, it will be alright? Well that felt like it was real to me too. I know it couldn't be, since Jack is dead."

"Derrick, no matter what you say, I believe this was no dream and that damn witch was telling us to get out of this cursed casino. Did you not feel the cold in the room when I woke you? How come it is not cold now?" convincingly she said.

"I don't know, Robyn. But I believe you. Let's get out of here and go get something to eat and then head home. Maybe we can make some sense out of this along the way."

In the Omelette House Derrick said, "Last night was one jammed pack party crowd. I worked my ass off."

"Yeah, so did I," countered Robyn.

Derrick seeing it was now almost one o'clock said, "Shit, we're supposed to be back at the Oasis by four. This is getting to be difficult. Working until four in the morning and going back the next day at four in the afternoon."

They finished eating, took two coffees to go, and decided to drive home.

On their way home Robyn just looked straight ahead saying nothing. Derrick asked, "What are you thinking about?"

She said slowly and firmly, "Maybe we should do what the damn witch suggested. Get out of this casino. You are working and coming home at 4am and turning around to go back at 4pm the next day. That will take a toll on your health. Plus giving twenty five percent of the money to Jack's mother. I can't help you much by working at the Starbite. When I do help on the weekends, like this one, I am exhausted come Sundays. On top of it all, putting up with those damn curses and now the witch saying if we stay we will die. I feel we should bail and take the $250,000 dollars Al said Jack would give us after the casino is sold."

Derrick now home, pulled his Forester into the garage. You take the coffee, and I'll get the mail and newspaper. Now inside he said, "Want to drink the coffee on the patio or just stay inside?"

Robyn said, "Let's just stay inside and talk a bit. Very soon we have to get ready for another big night at the Oasis."

Derrick heard what Robyn was saying and offered his response. "It was just days ago, Robyn, that we decided to give this casino two or three more months for us to try and work everything out. I know you are concerned about hearing that damn witch saying we will die if we don't get out. She told me that same thing at her home. This is still the middle of November. We have only been at this for less than three months. Why don't we just give this unbelievable, once in a lifetime opportunity, a couple of more months. Come the end of January, if things are still hectic and we continue having the curses, we can then decide to throw in the towel."

"I understand what you are saying, Derrick. But why did I see that damn witch last night?"

"I really don't know, Robyn. But I don't think we should give up now. Let's give it a shot for two more months. Don't we have another best dressed cowgirl contest tonight?"

"Yes we do, best sexy dressed cowgirl contest," Robyn said.

"Then let us think about that," Derrick said.

"We still have to address getting more help for Friday and Saturdays. Plus we need to find out how we can help our slow weekdays and nights," added Derrick. Robyn suggested, "If you are willing to keep going, yes, it looks to me like we need another gaming pit supervisor for weekend nights. Having just one is too demanding, especially when he needs to take a break. That is when you need to jump in, keeping you away from everything else."

"You are right, Robyn. We could use another supervisor. I will look into that."

"Now what about the weekdays and nights? Do you have any ideas?" she asked. "Maybe you could come up with some type of promotion or incentive. I thought about having a band on Wednesday nights. Not the expensive ones we have on the weekends, but a decent type of band," he suggested.

Robyn listening thought, "How about a rock band? We could feature Rock'n'Roll on Wednesday nights?"

"I like that. Country and Western on the weekends and Rock'n'Roll on Wednesdays.

"Good idea, Robyn. Now let's get ready for tonight.

Running a little late, they arrived about 4:30. Steve kind of thought they would be late because of the wild action they had all weekend. "Don't need to apologize for being a little late, Derrick. I know how demanding last night was. That cowgirl contest went over real BIG," added Steve.

"Yeah, and you know what Robyn said?" offered Derrick.

"What?"

"She said maybe we should have a best dressed cowboy hunk contest."

"Why not? Just you guys get to get your jolly's on? How about us girls?" asked Robyn.

"That sure sounds like Robyn. I don't know about that, though."

"Me either. But I do know we need to address some areas fast. I would like to talk to you about them tomorrow or if you can hang around for a few minutes now."

Steve said, "Derrick, I plan to help Robyn register the contestants and leave right after the contest. So, what's on your mind?"

"Steve, we need help on Friday and Saturday nights. I think we need another supervisor. One is just not enough."

"I think, in fact, I know you are right about that, Derrick. You know what I did on those nights before you came on?"

"What Steve?"

"I used Sam as a supervisor. She knows all the games and can record players cards and handle comps. Everything a supervisor needs to do, she can do it."

Derrick said, "Why don't we just make Sam a supervisor and bring in another part time dealer?"

"I was suggesting that to Jack but he just wanted to work it out the way it was. I felt I could not do that when he died, as the lawyer Al said no changes could be made. So, yes, I think that would work out great."

Derrick asked, "I will run this by Al on Monday. Do you think I should ask Sam tonight?"

"You mean to supervise tonight?" asked Steve.

"No, I don't think that would be fair. I just thought if we have any time, like on her break, I could feel her out," said Derrick.

"Feel her out?" smiled Steve.

"You know what I mean, Steve."

"Sure, I think she would be honored to hear something like that," offered Steve. "Also Steve, we need to do something about how slow it is during the weekdays," mentioned Derrick. He then went on, "I asked Robyn to try and come up with some type of promotion or incentive. Right out of the gate she suggested having a Rock'n'Roll band on Wednesday nights."

"That sounds interesting. A rock band on Wednesday and Country and Western on the weekends. I think that would go over, especially a rock band. That appeals to the younger crowd who doesn't mind staying up late on weekdays," added Steve.

Derrick asked, "Can I count on you, Steve, to get that rock band and look for another part time dealer for Friday and Saturday nights?"

"That would not be a problem. I will get on that Monday. All of our entertainment comes from the Artist On Call Club in Vegas."

"Thanks, Steve. Is everything in order for tonight?"

"Yes. No call offs. If your night is anything like last night, I probably won't see you until five o'clock tomorrow," said Steve.

Saturday night Western Days was just getting started. The dealers were all in place. Slots were ringing and table games had eight players. It looked like it was going to be a good night. Derrick went to the pit and said to Sam, "When you go on break, look me up. I need to talk with you."

At 7:00 Sam went on break. She found Derrick and they headed to the break room, as this was a good time just before it became busy. On the way, he picked up three coffees; one for Sam and him and one for Robyn. As they passed the lodge registration desk, Robyn was getting ready to sign up cowgirl contestants. She knew that Derrick was going to ask Sam to be a supervisor. She thanked

Derrick for the coffee.

Instead of the break room, Derrick took Sam into the office. "Am I in some kind of trouble or something," asked Sam.

Derrick smiled saying, "Absolutely not. Sam, you are a very good dealer that knows all the games. I know you helped out Steve with supervising the games in the past. How would you like being our second supervisor on Friday and Saturday nights?"

Sam seemed surprised, "That certainly has thrown me back. That would be great. Thanks, Derrick. But I have one question. How am I going to make up the money being a supervisor? You know, on those two nights, the toke is very damn good."

Derrick continued, "I was thinking more of a dual rate supervisor. So you could supervise mainly and fill in dealing when necessary. Your pay would always be what the dealers make plus extra as a supervisor."

Sam was pleased and said, "That I can live with. Thanks again, Derrick. When do you want me to start this?"

"How about next weekend, providing I can get another part time dealer for those days?" he said.

"That would be okay with me," Sam said and added, "I have a guy, Chris, that is a good dealer and works with me part time at the Silver Coin. He is looking to pick up some days, and I think he would jump at working weekend nights here."

"Great Sam! Can you have him give me a call?"

"I will give him a call tomorrow," said Sam. "You have made my day!" said Sam as she gave him a peck on the cheek and went back to the pit.

Saturday panned out well. It was not as wild as Friday, but still a fun crowd that liked the Western Days theme, especially the best sexy dressed cowgirl contest. The gaming take was a little better this night as there were more higher stake bets made. Simply put, a very successful two nights of action.

Derrick was tired from the wild weekend, but he still was able to get back to the Oasis by 3:30 on Sunday. Robyn stayed home to leisurely get the house in order and relax for her regular weekday job. She would try and come up with some ideas to increase business at the Oasis for weekdays.

Derrick met Steve at the cashier. "How was last night after I left?" asked Steve. "It stayed packed up to two, then tapered off. The table games must have done well from what I saw," implied Derrick.

Steve completed all of the income reports saying, "Table games really did well. Excellent take and the toke rate was very big. You must of had some players betting big?"

"We sure did. That is what we need to focus on going forward," replied Derrick.

Steve mentioned, "I received a phone call from a guy named Chris. He asked for you saying something about dealing."

"Yes, that is the guy Sam referred to replace her on the weekend nights," said Derrick.

"So, I gathered asking Sam to be a supervisor went well?" Steve asked.

"Yeah it did. She will be our dual rate supervisor."

"That is great. Sam should work out fine. Here is the phone number for Chris. I believe he said you could call anytime." Steve continued, "You can check the reports in the office. I think everything should be in order and up to date. Jerry will be in tomorrow to get the month ending reports ready for finalizing on Wednesday."

"I am glad you guys are on top of this stuff. The hours I'm working would make it tough for me to do it. I'll review the reports with Jerry on Wednesday," said Derrick.

After Steve left, Derrick went to the office to look at the weekend figures and reports. He called Chris and made a connection. "Hello, this is Chris."

"Chris, this is Derrick Burns from the Lucky Oasis."

"Hi Derrick. Sam asked me to call you about working as a part time dealer on the weekend nights," said Chris.

"Yes, that is correct. What type of games do you deal? What is your current work schedule?" Derrick asked.

Chris answered, "I deal all games except baccarat. I am working Tuesday, Wednesday, and Thursday nights right now. I would like to pick up Friday and Saturday if possible."

Derrick said, "Sounds good to me. I usually like to interview, in person, those applying for a job. However, Sam has given you high ratings, and we value Sam's opinion here, so I am offering you Friday and Saturday nights to deal for us." "Yes, that would be fantastic. When do you want me to start?" asked Chris.

"This coming weekend too soon?"

"Not at all. What time do I start?"

"The shift for both nights is 6pm to 3am. But I need you to come in at five to sign some paperwork and copy your badge," said Derrick.

"That would work out just fine. See you next Friday. I will be there by five," agreed Chris.

Friday, after Thanksgiving, was hopping again with the band Silver Spurs. Derrick thought it might not be so busy being Black Friday and all, but the talk is out there that Western Days, along with the best sexy dressed cowgirl contest, was the place to be.

Sam did a good job of supervising, and Chris proved to be an excellent dealer. The pressure that Derrick experienced on the weekend nights was gone. He was able to walk around and see that all areas were functioning properly. This is what he envisioned and what he enjoyed doing.

This was the third weekend for Western Days and the second for the cowgirl contest. The acceptance and huge crowds dictated that this would be the theme going forward.

Next week, on Wednesday, was Rock'n'Roll day. Steve was able to get a rock band called "Rigit." They have a good reputation for playing the current hits and the cost was reasonable. As for the weekdays, Robyn was toying around with free slot credits for a certain amount of play. She had not worked out all the details, but hoped to in a few days.

Chapter 16

SPIRTUAL CONTACTS

Sunday nights were always very slow. This Sunday it was dead. Occasionally a player or two would stroll in for a little while, but basically there were not too many players.

It was December fourth. Ten minutes after Derrick arrived at 4:00, the music stopped and the death, dull, loud bell sounded, DONG. "Son-of-a-bitch," he blurted out. Yellowish smoke started coming in from the air vents. Now he knew for sure they would go off on the fourth of every month. DONG. This damn bell would go off every minute for an hour.

DONG. Derrick got an idea. He told the Lounge and Eatery to stand by the cash register. One person was at the bar and no one at the Eatery. DONG. He then went to the pit and told the two dealers to put the tray cover over the gaming chips and not to remove until instructed. DONG. He dashed over to the control room and pulled the main power switch down (off). The entire casino went dark and the generator kicked on. DONG. "DAMN IT!" he said. The death bell still sounded with all the power shut off and the generator on. "I can't fucking believe this!" he shouted out. DONG. Derrick turned the power back on and went back to the pit.

At 5:00 the death bell stopped. Derrick was in the lounge drinking a shot and beer. He needed that to calm his nerves. He thanked Bob, the bartender, for the drink saying, "If it is this slow at midnight, go ahead and close down."

Derrick was up in the office when Robyn called. "How's things?" she asked.

"Very slow. You know what happened at 4:00?"

"What?"

"Those damn death bells and smoke, that's what happened. One every minute for sixty minutes. I even tried shutting all the power off. The generator came on and so did those shitty bells," he said.

Robyn feeling sorry for him said, "Sorry you had to go through that again."

Derrick added, "To calm my nerves, I had a shot and beer. I feel better now. How are you doing?"

She said, "I'm okay. I fixed up some stuff around the house. Also, how does this sound for the weekdays and nights as a promotion? We issue the Lucky Oasis its first players card. On your first visit using your new players card, you get back fifty percent of all your losses up to $100. After that, you earn credits for cash back or comps for food and lodging. I will see if the players card can be tied in with the Starbrite for double impact."

"That sounds real good, Robyn. Go ahead and work out all the details and let me know when we can start that up. I will tell the dealers so they know we are trying to increase players. Also, I am staying here tonight. I will be meeting Jerry tomorrow on all the reports we are filing. Don't forget Wednesday is our Rock'n'Roll day. The band 'Rigit' will play from 8pm to 1am."

"Oh shit, that's right. Well, I will be there until about ten, then I will have to leave.

Love you, hun."

"Love you back."

Derrick made up the next day's banks in the counting room. So when Steve arrived tomorrow, he could just put them out to get the day started. This would give him more time to work on the reports with Jerry. He noticed that there were four players in the pit. Three playing blackjack and one playing roulette. So he went down to supervise.

Derrick introduced himself to the players. "Is there anything I can get you guys? One of the guys said he noticed the bar was closed but would like a beer. The other three guys said the same. "Bud or Bud Light?" asked Derrick. Three said Bud Light and one said a Bud. Derrick brought over the beers and all the guys nodding their heads said, "Thanks, man!" Derrick thought this could help build players good will.

At twelve thirty, two people were left playing blackjack and maybe four or five people playing slots. That was not bad for this late on Sunday. He decided to close the lodge and eatery. He kept one dealer and sent two home. The two of them could handle whatever players they would get the rest of the night.

At 2:45 Derrick was talking with the security guard and said, "We have not had one player here since about two. Time to close this place. There was just one dealer on hand as he closed him out. Derrick locked the last door as the security guard left. He put the last cash box in the counting room and went to his sleeping room in the lodge.

While Derrick was sleeping, he woke up being very cold. He heard a muffled dungeon type sound. "Derrick, get out of this casino." Looking up he saw a transparent figure. Once again, this floating see through figure said, "Derrick get out of this casino before it is too late." As he squinted his eyes he realized the vision looked like Wendy, the witch. The image faded slowly away. He looked at the clock; it was 7:30. He got out of bed, used the bathroom, turned on the lights and looked around.

There was no one but him in the room. He turned off the lights, jumped back in bed, pulling all the covers to his neck. He wondered. Did I have a dream or did I really see what I saw? Then he remembered what Robyn said she saw in this very room several days ago. The same image with the same coldness. This could not have been a dream but must have been what he heard and saw. Closing his eyes, tossing and turning, he finally fell back to sleep.

After waking up around eleven, he realized the room temperature was comfortable, not cold. His thoughts were on the vision and words he had seen and heard.

After dressing, he decided not to tell anyone what he saw and heard. He even would keep it, for now, from Robyn.

He went into the casino directly to the Eatery. He said good morning to Joanne, working the eatery, and asked for a chocolate donut and black coffee. He sat down noticing four older guys talking. These senior men usually came in every morning to talk and have breakfast. He waved to them, and they did the same. Now he decided to go over to the four senior men. "I just want to thank you for coming to the Oasis Eatery in the mornings. Here is a little note that will allow you all to have breakfast on me. By the way, I am Derrick Burns, the manager." They all thanked him for the comp. One of the men said, "We like this place and have been coming here for years. We all liked Jack and was sorry to hear what happened to him."

"Yes, me too," said Derrick. "Jack was my best friend. In his passing, he asked my wife, Robyn, and me to carry on and manage his casino complex."

"Well, from my stand point, you appear to be just the right person to do that," said one of the men.

"Thank you again. Stay as long as you want," suggested Derrick.

Derrick picked up his donut and coffee heading to a table. Steve saw Derrick in the Eatery. "Hey," Steve said walking over, "So you stayed here last night?"

"Yes I did, Steve. Knowing I was going to review the reports with Jerry today, I decided just to stay here. I just needed to get something to eat and have some coffee before going up. Those damn bells went off again last evening at four and stayed on until five."

"So they are now happening every month on the fourth," stated Steve.

"Looks like it, Steve."

"That's too bad. When you get finished, I'll go with you to see Jerry, just in case you have any questions," Steve offered.

Jerry Duncan was a good accountant. All the reports were completely finished and ready to go in. Derrick thanked Jerry for his service and offered his assistance if needed.

Derrick said to Steve they would be offering a new players card very soon. Robyn was finishing up the details, trying to include it in with the Starbrite. Steve seemed to think that a players card might be a good idea.

They both went down to the pit and informed the dealer's about the new players card coming. Derrick assured the dealers that they are doing everything they can to increase player activity. This, he hoped, would stop the rumor that some of the week day dealers were planning to leave.

Before Steve left for the day, Derrick reminded him of Rock'n'Roll Wednesday.

Steve asked Derrick to look at the marquee. It showed, Wed. Rock'n'Roll, Band Rigit 8pm, Western Days Fri. & Sat., Band 4 Aces+1 Queen. Derrick said, "Good thing we have a four line marquee. Thanks Steve, looks good. Have a good night."

When Derrick arrived Wednesday, Steve informed him, "I'm going to hang out here so I can observe that Rock'n'Roll band 'Rigit' tonight. So, if you don't need me for anything right now, I will check out the Oasis Lounge. I'll go see if Don needs any help with the supplies and such before Burt shows up."

"Sounds like a plan, Steve. Robyn will also come by for a while. I'll be in the lodge office, if you need something."

Robyn came in right at shift changes. She did not want to bother Derrick until he was able to get the evening dealers set up. Steve talked with Robyn until Derrick joined them. All three went to the Eatery for something to eat. Robyn said, "The marquee looks good; hope we have a good crowd."

"Steve set up the marquee. He also had a small article in (What's Happening Town)," stated Derrick adding, "Hope that will be enough, especially since I have five dealers tonight."

The band Rigit started setting up at seven. By seven thirty they were ready to go. There were about thirty people in the lounge. Derrick said to Robyn, "So far, this does not look too promising." He looked over at the gaming pit and saw only four players.

Robyn said, "Relax, it is not even eight o'clock. Let's see how it looks by nine." The band's second set started at nine twenty with the lounge fairly crowded. It wasn't like weekend nights, but for the first Rock'n'Roll night, not bad. Rigit was loud and very good at playing the current hits. The young crowd seemed to like this band a lot. The gaming area had enough players to keep all the dealers active. Not all the seats were filled but much better action than what Wednesday nights had before.

Robyn and Steve left around ten thirty. As soon as the clock struck midnight with the band still on break, all the lights started flickering on and off, on and off until the place went completely dark. Within seconds, the generator kicked on. All the lights came back on, but that ungodly organ sound, also came on. Derrick told the dealers to continue dealing, as long as there was light. He told them bring up their tray cover if the lights go off. He then went to the Oasis Lounge. With that ugly organ sound, he told the band to stay on break until he could get it stopped.

The generator stopped and the electric went back on. Immediately the lights started flickering on and off along with the organ sounds. Both at the same time! "Son of a bitch," snarled Derrick. The lights flickering DID NOT stop after twenty minutes like before. Derrick did not know what to do. He noticed many people walking out. He went over to the band and said, "We are having some technical difficulties. Let me suggest calling it quits for tonight. Sorry guys." They understood and packed up with lights flickering and spooky organ sounds in the background. Derrick paid the band and said, "When we get our system fixed, I will give you guys a call."

Derrick told the bartender to close and did the same for the Eatery. Then he went to the gaming pit. Now there still were four players not giving up. He watched the dealers trying to deal with lights flickering on and off. Finally, he said to the the dealers to close down. "Sorry everyone. It seems we are experiencing some technical difficulties We have to close." The players colored up their chips and took them to the cashier.

As the lights kept flickering on and off, along with that shitty organ sound, Derrick asked the security officer to be sure to escort out the remaining players. When the last person was gone, he locked all the doors and said good night to the officer. It was now just five minutes past 1am.

As Derrick was gathering all the money and toke boxes, the flickering lights and organ sounds stopped. He went to the cashier to be sure it was securely locked. On his way to picking up the cash boxes from the Oasis Lounge and Eatery, the whole place started getting cold. It was then that the transparent vision of a figure appeared, and hearing an echo sounding voice saying, *"I told you to get out of this casino. The curses will continue to get stronger and more often. Get out of this casino before it is too late."* Derrick tried to speak to the vision that he knew was Wendy. "Wendy, Wendy, why...what's the big rush in all...." Breaking in the vision said, *"Get out of this casino. This is your last warning."* He sat down, shaken and worried, staring up at the vision as it slowly disappeared. After just sitting there for a period of time, he finished putting all the cash boxes in the counting room. He drove home at 1:30am.

When Derrick got home he wrote a note to Robyn. We need to talk asap about the Oasis. We had two curses starting at midnight and they did not stop. I closed the casino at 12:30. I also got a vision from Wendy that said to get out of this casino.

He decided to sleep on the couch so as not to wake Robyn.

Robyn awoke and took a shower. She dressed and went into the kitchen. She noticed Derrick sleeping on the couch. Thinking that was kind of strange, she quietly went into the kitchen and found his note on the table. After reading it she wondered if she should wake him or not. She decided to make her breakfast, trying to make as little noise as possible.

It was Thursday morning and Derrick woke up just as Robyn finished her breakfast. "Sorry if I woke you," she said.

"You didn't, I just needed to use the bathroom. Hold on, before going to work," he said.

Robyn cleaned up the kitchen as Derrick came back. "Sit down, please sit down a minute," he suggested.

"I know you have to go to work, but you have to hear this." Robyn said, "I saw your note."

Derrick, looking stern and worried said, "The lights started flickering and this time all the lights went out. The casino was completely dark for a couple of seconds before the generator came on. That's when that fucking, eerie organ sound started. The lights came back on flickering again along with the organ sound. It went on and on and on. People were walking out in droves. That's when I closed the casino. When everyone was gone, the casino turned very cold and there she was, Wendy, the fucking witch. I know it was Wendy, even though you could see through her. She was floating around saying, "Get out of this casino; this is your final warning." Robyn could see that Derrick was almost out of breath and shook up. She went over to the couch sitting next to him and said, "What are you going to do?" He went on like he didn't even hear her, "This was the *second* time in a week that the witch appeared to me." "Second time?" she asked.

"Yea, last Sunday night when I stayed at the lodge, Wendy appeared saying the same thing, "Get out of this casino before it is too late." We also had those damn death bells then too. I didn't want to say anything at that time because Rock'n'Roll night was coming on Wednesday. I wanted to see how that played out without any concerns or worries."

Robyn said, "Pour yourself some coffee. I'm going to call in sick today. I just can't go to work when you are so upset and getting these threats. We need to discuss this fully."

"Oh Robyn, go to work. We can discuss this when you get home. You have taken a lot of time off, as it is," he said.

"Fuck that Derrick, this is sounding like it is becoming out-of-control. I need to be with you now. We need to discuss this whole thing, NOW!" Robyn said firmly. Derrick sat down at the kitchen table with his head down. Robyn returned, after calling off sick and said, "We are going to talk this out and decide what the hell we are going to do *TODAY*. I know we said let's give this a couple more months, but now the curses are more frequent, getting stronger and several sightings from that damn witch, saying get the fuck out."

"That is about what is happening, Robyn. I can't stop any of these curses. People are leaving the place and, I think it's starting to drive me nuts," he said.

Robyn poured herself another cup of coffee thinking, "Remember what Al said when we told him about these damn curses. If we decided not to continue managing the Lucky Oasis, for whatever reason, we could turn the whole operation back to him. When the place is sold, we would get two hundred and fifty thousand dollars. I think we should give that some serious thought right now."

Derrick got up, put two pieces of bread in the toaster, refilled his coffee, buttered his toast and returned to the table. "Well, fucking say something," said Robyn. He sort of smiled and said, "I'm thinking, Robyn. I'm thinking that, that may be our only choice. If that witch is adding more curses and even changing curses, how soon is it before the fucking death curse kicks in? She has given us several warnings now. We better damn well take them serious. I feel like taking a gun and telling that fucking witch to stop the curses or I'll blow her fucking head off."

"Derrick," Robyn said with a sinister look, "Do you think that would work?"

"Huuh, probably not. She might melt that damn gun into my hand, or something.

"Why don't we call Al, as soon as it is nine o'clock, tell him what has taken place and that we can no longer run the Oasis," suggested Robyn.

Derrick looked sad while he agreed. "Sure you don't want to go work? You still have time; it is just 8:30."

"No, I have already called in and I want to be with you today. We need to do this together," she said.

Derrick called Al at ten minutes after nine. They said Al was in court all morning and would not be available until the afternoon. Derrick said, "This is an emergency, and I need to talk with him as soon as he is available. Please have him call me."

Resting on the couch with the newspaper folded on his lap, Derrick's phone rang. Seeing it was from Al he answered, "Hi Al, thanks for calling me. We have a situation." Derrick went on informing Al, in complete detail, of what has been going on and that he and Robyn needed to give up the conditional ownership to the Lucky Oasis Casino.

Al understod what Derrick was saying and was disappointed in the unfortunate circumstances. He was also concerned about their health. So he suggested, "Write a short letter saying, due to the many working hours required and for health reasons, we can no longer continue being owners of the Lucky Oasis Casino and Lodge. Do not put anything in the letter about spells, curses or witchcraft. Both of you sign it, with your full legal names, and bring that letter to me. I will notarize it and use it with the necessary documents I will need to prepare." Derrick asked, "Can we bring the letter today?'

"Absolutely. I will be here at the office until 4:30," Al replied.

Robyn left her computer and was listening to the conversation when Derrick asked Al, "What about the Lucky Oasis? I mean, I'm supposed to be there today at four. There really is no one else to manage it as Steve leaves at four. Would you advise me going there or not?"

Al thought for a minute then said, "It is difficult for me to say. You have said that this witch wanted you out, as owners. By you handing in this letter you, in fact, are resigning ownership. If you agree to stay on as a manager, I do not know if the witch would be satisfied with that. I'm not an expert on witchcraft. Maybe you should give her a call and say you have given up ownership and that you have been asked to stay on as a manager until a purchaser is found. See what response you get. If she still holds you responsible, you might want to re-think continuing to work there. If that is the case, let me know quickly."

"That makes sense. I think that's what I'll do. If the damn witch has no problem with me being a manager, I will stay on until there are new owners," said Derrick. Al also added, "If you do agree to manage the Lucky Oasis, you would receive a salary, with no benefits. The choice is strictly up to you. I have to go now. There is another matter that needs my attention. Good luck with all this, Derrick."

"Thank you Al. See you later," Derrick said and hung up.

Derrick got himself and Robyn a beer. He explained the entire conversation to her. "So what do you think?" She didn't have to think long and said, "Looks like you need to call that fucking witch and hear what the hell she has to say first." Derrick agreed, and that's what he did.

Wendy answered, "You called Wendy."

"Hi Wendy. This is Derrick Burns from the Lucky Oasis Casino. I just wanted to let you know that I have resigned today as the owner."

"Glad you got the message," Wendy said.

"One more thing, Wendy. They have asked me to stay on as a manager just until they get the place sold. You don't have any problems with that, do you?" asked Derrick.

Wendy said, "You are very stubborn and reckless. As long as you, or anyone, has anything to do with operating that damn casino, they will be held to the curses.

Does that answer your question?"

Derrick was amazed at how cold and thoughtless she was and said, "You know, Wendy, I called you in good faith. Just to tell you I was giving up the request of my dead best friend; giving up the once in a lifetime opportunity he gave me just to satisfy you. Instead you have demonstrated you are one fucking evil piece of shit. I hope you rot in hell." She banged the phone down ending the call.

"Those were some real choice words you just made," said Robyn.

"That fucking bitch said *anyone* operating the Oasis is held responsible. That means not only me, but you and Steve. She is just one bitter, mean, frustrated bitch. It does not matter if you are the owner or not.

Just running the place has her all pissed off," said Derrick very disturbed."

"Now don't get your balls in an uproar, Derrick. I do not think we should continue with the Oasis. Let's go into the office and compose the letter Al said we need to write. When we give him the letter, we'll just say it's not going to work out and he will have to find someone else to manage the Lucky Oasis," Robyn said with conviction.

"I guess you are right, Robyn. It is just so frustrating knowing we could run a real casino. Our best friend, Jack, wanting us to continue on with his casino. Now, with this fucking witch and her curses, have to give up on this wonderful opportunity. This makes me so damn mad! I guess we should type out that resignation letter," he suggested very disgusted.

As they went into the office to compose the letter, they heard someone talking.

"Derrick. Robyn. Come here."

"Did you hear that, Robyn?" asked Derrick.

"Yeah. Sounded like someone calling us, in our living room." They both went in the living room and stopped in their tracks. "Hi guys," a floating transparent Jack said. "What in God's good name is happening?' asked Derrick. Robyn stunned, added, "Is that really you, Jack?"

"Sort of," the see through figure said. "Don't be afraid, I am just a spirit. I needed to see you both. I wanted to thank you for running my casino and helping out with my mother." They both sat down, in awe, with their mouths open on the couch as Jack floated around. "I knew you would do a good job of running and protecting the Lucky Oasis. That is why I chose you both. I also know what has been happening to you with the curses." Jack floated around stating, "Those curses have been there for some time. When my dad died, he could not do anything in the spirit world to stop the curses. So when the timing was right, I lost my earthly life as well. Now that I am in the spirit world, I have been given the power from the Almightly to correct this evil. Yes, I can stop those curses that have been haunting you both. But first, you have to believe."

"Believe what?" asked Robyn.

"You must believe that I can stop the curses. If you do, you will need to contribute $1,000 to a worthy charity--like the Red Cross, Saint Jude's Children's

Hospital or any good deserving chairity of your choice." Jack floated around again.

Robyn, in amazement blurted out, "Are you seeing and hearing this, Derrick?" "Yes, Robyn." As his eyes moved with Jack floating around. Jack continued, "The contribution must be made within the next ten days from today. If you do this, all the curses will be lifted except the death curse. The death curse will be lifted when you contribute $1,000 to another worthwhile charity of your choice within 60 days from today."

Derrick looking at Robyn in some weird way said, "Why do contributions Jack, to a charity, have to do with all this?"

Jack floating back and forth said, "I understand that you both have been good, upstanding citizens trying to do what is right. But there is one thing I've been told you have been lax with, and that's helping out with charity contributions. So the Almighty has given me the power to take away the evil curses set on you, providing you recognize the need to help out charities. It is as simple as that."

"Wow!" said Derrick. "All the curses will be removed if we just start contributing to charities. I hope we are not just sleeping and that this is all a dream."

Robyn starring at the floating Jack asked, "What about in the meantime Jack. I mean, until we make a contribution to a charity, will the curses continue, or what?"

Jack looking at them both said, "This is not a dream guys. This for real. When Wendy lost her husband, she turned to the dark side with her crafts. If you believe what I have said, and you contribute to the charities in the time frame mentioned, there will be no more evil curses on the Oasis or you. Right now all the curses on the Lucky Oasis have been suspended for the next ten days."

"I believe, Jack. I believe. What took you so long in addressing these curses?" asked Derrick.

Jack's image and voice started to fade, as he tells them, "Sorry guys, I have to go but this is not a dream. The Almighty works in strange ways. I was not able to work on the curses until now. Please believe in me. Make your contributions and the curses will be no more. Do not write the letter or resign. Thank you both." Jack's image was gone.

"Thanks, Jack. Thanks, Jack!" shouted Derrick not knowing if Jack heard him. "WOW!" said Robyn. "I am glad I didn't go to work today. Now what are you going to do?"

Derrick said, "Pinch me, Robyn." So she did. "Ouch! I felt that. We are awake. We are not dreaming. I'm going to believe Jack. You saw and heard him. The curses will be gone. Don't you think we should continue on, like he said?"

"That is what Jack said," answered Robyn.

Derrick added, "It's like his spirit overcame the witches spirit. That's good enough for me. We don't need to write a damn resignation letter. What we need to do is write a check for $1,000 to the Red Cross, NOW. He asked Robyn to make out the check."

Derrick went over to the refrigerator and took out a Bud and Bud Light. "Here," he said. Giving the Bud Light to Robyn. "Let's drink on this. This is unbelievable!" Robyn said, "You are not fucking kidding. What a change in this day!"

"You know Robyn, all the supernatural visits from the witch occured at the Oasis, said Derrick. Let's plan on spending Friday and Saturday nights at the Oasis. Just to see if that witch will appear or not. I'm not saying I do not believe in Jack, but I am just curious to see if that damn witch will say we won or goodbye or whatever." "I think you're nuts. I think the witch is pissed off. But I'll stay at the Oasis with you this Friday and Saturday," she said.

"I will be going over to the Lucky Oasis after I finish my beer. I will complete my shift tonight. I will call Al first, and explain what has happened."

Robyn said, "After that, I'll go with you to the Oasis in my own car. We can tell Steve what just took place and celebrate with a drink. On the way, I will mail the check to the Red Cross.

Chapter

17

END OF THE CURSES

It was 3:45 when Derrick showed up at the Lucky Casino. When he caught up with

Steve he cheerfully asked, "Can you stick around for a little while?"

"Sure. What's up?" asked Steve.

"Let's go to the lounge so we can order a drink. Robyn will join us briefly. We got some good news," an upbeat Derrick said.

Steve asked, "What's the good news?"

"First we get the drinks. Have anything you want, Steve. Derrick ordered a whiskey sour for himself and a frozen strawberry daiquiri for Robyn. Just then

Robyn showed up. With drinks in hand, they went to a booth.

"Hi beautiful," said Steve.

"Hi Steve. Did Derrick tell you anything yet?"

"No. I am anxious to hear what you have to say," a curious Steve said.

"First Robyn, let me tell Steve what took place here last night." She nodded.

Derrick explained all the details of the two curses happening at the same time, and that he had to close the casino. Before driving home, I had a vision from the witch saying to get out of the casino. This is your last warning."

He then told Steve about contacting the lawyer, Al. That they were going to write a resignation letter whe .."

Robyn breaks in, "That's when, believe it or not, we both received a vision from Jack. He told us he was able to remove the curses from his casino and to continue on. NO MORE CURSES, Steve!"

"O my God! You actually saw Jack? That is unbelievable! You sure you guys were not dreaming this?"

"No, no, no Steve, not a dream. This is fucking real. Robyn even pinched me. Even though Jack was a spirit, we believe what Jack said and now we are fully engaged. We will be moving forward, with your help, to make Jack's casino a real success!" said Derrick excitedly! He also added, "We have noticed how well you have pitched in Steve, helping us keep Jack's casino moving forward. So we value you and want you to continue working here, and we will upgrade your salary very shortly."

Steve said, " Thank you very much. I enjoy working for you guys and finally, a normal operating casino. No more fucking curses! This is just unbelieveably good news. Yes it is Steve," said Robyn. "Now we can have a 'hot cowboy hunk contest." They all had a laugh and made a cheer, holding up their drinks.

Friday and Saturday nights were jam packed. Western Days continued to be a big hit with the locals. The guys especially liked the best sexy dressed cowgirl contest. When Robyn mentioned that they were adding the best cowboy hunk contest, the girls were just as wild and noisy as the guys.

During each night while Derrick and Robyn slept, there was no visit from the witch. There still was that apprehensiveness in them, until the curse dates and times came about. It is not that they didn't believe Jack, but they just wanted to experience those dates and times for real verification. It starts with the 4th of the month for the death bells and smoke, the full moon at midnight with the flickering lights, and the new curse every Thursday at 4pm of eerie organ sounds. When those times came and went without any curses, they all celebrated and said, HALLELUJAH!!

The next three and one half years were very productive for the Lucky Oasis. So much so that Robyn left her event planning job at the Starbrite. She and Derrick worked full time making the casino a fun and exciting place to visit. The Western Days and Rock'n'Roll Wednesdays continued to be very popular. Robyn, getting her own way again, added the best hot cowboy contest along with the best sexy dressed cowgirl contest. The girls were just as loud as the guys when that happened. Jack's mom passed away and the Burns handled liquidating her estate. All proceeds were sent to Jack's designated charities. They were now freed from taking out twenty-five percent of the profits for Jack's mom.

Also, they added eight gas pumps for those traveling back to California. Fuel was much cheaper in Nevada than California, and that proved very popular and profitable. More travelers stopped in for gas and spent money on food and even some gaming. Robyn's player card, Oasis Rewards, was becoming popular and actually was increasing daily play. Steve proved to me a valuable employee. The revenue they earned for themselves, after expenses, proved adequate.

In the back of their minds, they still were nervous about today, which was April 4. That would mark the four years since Jack's death. Derrick, Robyn and Steve planned on being extra cautious throughout the day. When it was almost 4pm, while standing near the front entrance, they heard a loud bang. Another bang. Followed by two more bangs. They all jumped. It was outside. Derrick grabbed Robyn wrapping his arms around her. Steve veered out the front door glass trying to see what was happening. Another bang. Steve now shaking his head with a smile said, "It is just an older car leaving the parking lot backfiring."

Derrick and Robyn relaxed with a sigh of relief. "Just a car backfiring," said Derrick. "On April 4th at 4pm. What are the odds?"

Robyn offered, "Maybe it's the fucking witch with a farewell jester."

Derrick and Steve just laughed.

They all went back getting ready for the days action. Everything went smoothly the rest of the day. No one lost their life. Finally, all the dates came to pass, and curses never occurred. The Lucky Oasis was free to operate without the fear of Wendy's curses, thanks to Jack Capano. His legacy would live on through his friends, Derrick and Robyn Burns.